Small House, Large World

Also by

Barbara M. Dickinson

A Rebellious House

Secrets from My Kitchen

Grandfather Jumper and the Cookie Eating Monsters
(a picture book for children)

Small House, Large World

A Novel

by Barbara M. Dickinson

Brunswick

Library of Congress Cataloging-in-Publication Data

Dickinson, Barbara M., 1933–
    Small house, large world : a novel / by Barbara M. Dickinson. -- 1st ed.
        p.   c.m.
    Sequel to: A rebellious house
    ISBN 1-55618-182-5 (pbk. : alk. paper)
    I. Title.
PS3554.I3238S53   1999
813'. 54--dc21   99–29306
                                         CIP

First Edition

Published in the United States of America

by

Brunswick Publishing Corporation
1386 Lawrenceville Plank Road
Lawrenceville, Virginia 23868
1-800-336-7154

For Billy, *ab imo pectore*,
with love and gratitude for sharing
both small house and large world.
Ars est celare artem.
Finis.

Acknowledgments

Words of appreciation are inadequate when thanking the many people responsible for the creation of this book. Nonetheless, I would like to thank the following, whose encouragement and criticism kept me on track: Jocey and Margery in Sussex, who sent me bits and pieces of England at my every request; Margaret Grayson and Scott Rogers, for their instant and precise translations; Charles Bray, for his sympathetic diagnosis of Father Charlie's mishap; Richard, for introducing me to Hummers; Marianne, Alan and Teresa, ever helpful, ever supportive; Lynn Eckman, for her wisdom and sharp eyes; Jane Kuhn and Jake Wheeler, for the privilege of traveling with them and being the model tour leaders that Rose hoped to emulate; Agnes Reid for her quotable quote.

Special thanks go to my daughter, Hilary Rogers, upon whose insight and perception I often depended and always trusted; and to my husband, for his patience and cheerful encouragement as he coaxed me toward the final page. I am indebted to you both.

And a heartfelt thank-you to my many readers, who kept asking, "When will we be hearing about Rose's Roamings?"

Bon Voyage! Enjoy the trip that you made possible!

BARBARA M. DICKINSON
April 1999

Wynfield Farms and its residents exist, alas, only in the heart and mind of the author. The cities and places of interest in this book, however, are very real and waiting to be explored.

~ ~ ~

I live in a small house
but my windows look out
on a very large world.

OLD CHINESE PROVERB

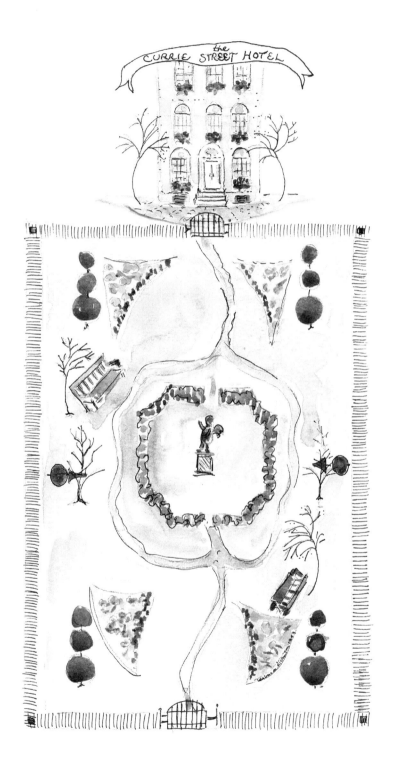

THE CURRIE STREET HOTEL
Founded 1899

Established in the final years of Queen Victoria's reign, the Currie Street Hotel has stood as a bastion of courtesy, comfort and civility for its many guests from every corner of the globe.

The Currie Street Hotel is unique in that it has remained an independent entity among the corporate-owned hotels throughout London. Responsibility for this goes to the tenacity and wisdom of the Apsell-Longley family. The Apsell-Longleys have been the sole owners of the Currie Street Hotel Foundation since 1899 when Mr. Hugh Apsell-Longley (later, Lord Apsell-Longley), a young gentleman of 23 years, purchased the one-half acre of land upon which portions of the original structure still stand. Originally a "Coaching Inn serving goodly food and meates" at lunch time only, Mr. Hugh Apsell-Longley gradually expanded both his land holdings and buildings. In 1912 the third and fourth floors of the old Currie were added, bringing the total number of guest rooms to 36. Over the years the Currie expanded until it reached the present number of 65 rooms, all with baths *en suite*. A complete renovation of the hotel was realized in 1991. There are no plans for further expansion.

It is now the fourth generation Apsell-Longley family that takes pride not only as proprietors of the Currie Street Hotel but in ensuring that it retains its elegance and old-fashioned charm in a world that has lost much of both.

Amenities of the Currie Street include Afternoon Tea for guests (Monday through Sunday, 3:30-5:30 P.M.), Lounge Bars for spirits, Private Dining Rooms for special functions, and the Main Dining Room (Monday-Sunday, 6:30-10 P.M.) for the convenience of all guests. With a wine list selected from the world's finest vineyards and a cosmopolitan menu reflecting the best of London's varied markets, the Currie Street Hotel has one of the best and most traditional dining rooms in all the city.

An enclosed garden across Currie Street fronts the main entrance of the hotel. Fragrant in Spring with *prunus tribola* and many species of English blossoms, the garden affords guests a gentle respite from city noises.

Though small in size, visitors soon realize that the Currie Street Hotel never forgets a guest. And it is hoped that guests, having once visited this venerable domain, never forget the warm welcome of the Currie Street Hotel.

~ ~ ~

1

It started with a hairbrush. One hairbrush and two feet of snow that fell on the Shenandoah Valley in less than forty-eight hours.

Rose smiled to herself, remembering February as if it were yesterday, not two months past. She pushed aside the heavy draperies and rested both hands on the window sill. Through a fringe of lime-colored leaves she could see the green and gated square below.

The light is different here. Somehow sharper. Even in the city there is a clarity we don't see at home.

Beyond the borders of the iron grille work that fenced in tidy clumps of shrubs and a dazzling display of early jonquils there were people walking along the sidewalk and cars whishing by rapidly.

The pocket-size plot was manicured to perfection, yet as welcoming as a pastoral hillside in spring. Two sturdy teak benches, protectively placed aside ornamental almond trees, beckoned visitors to sit and soak up the sun in this green sliver of solitude.

Primroses, hyacinths, and wallflowers struggled for dominance in the crowded and carefully turned loamy borders.

Ah, wallflowers! Now I know I am back in England. That evocative English scent. I remember it from ... how many Aprils ago? Forty-three? It was Oxford when I first saw them. I recall thinking England had gone flower-mad; the sheer numbers and colors of the flowers dazzled me. The beds in the colleges' court-yards overflowed with these tough little buggers. Why couldn't some smart perfumery bottle that elusive, lovely delicate aroma that is peculiarly English wallflower?

And across Brompton Road—my favorite Boots the Chemist and the successor to this miserable hairbrush. I'll bury it before Ellie teases me unmercifully.

Rose McNess giggled in spite of herself, thinking once again of the domino effect of her disreputable hairbrush.

A soft knock at the door interrupted her daydreams.

"Coming, coming," she whispered hoarsely, hurrying to avoid waking Ellie Johnson who lay sprawled and snoring across the twin bed.

Opening the door she was surprised to find Cyril, the aged hotel butler. He was gingerly balancing a laden tea tray in white gloved hands. "Oh, Cyril, how really kind of you," she whispered enthusiastically. "Here, let me take it; my friend is sleeping soundly and I don't want to wake her. What a lovely thing for you to do, Cyril. Tea will just hit the spot this morning."

"Welcome back to the Currie, Mrs. McNess." His response was formal, mannered, but warm. "My deepest pleasure to greet you once again. Please let us know if there is anything we may do to enhance your stay with us."

"Thank you, Cyril. One thing only: tea this afternoon, in that small room, off the Lounge. I did ask you about that, didn't I, when we arrived this morning? Seems so long ago I can't for the life of me remember what I told you or what I meant to tell you. Did I mention it, Cyril?"

"Of course, Madam. You said to lay on tea for eight. Is the number still correct?"

"Eight is correct, Cyril. Thank you. About four this afternoon."

"Yes, Madam."

Bowing silently, gracefully, Cyril closed the door noiselessly after Rose.

"Who was that, Rose?" came a groggy voice from beneath the duvet.

"Oh, Ellie, I was trying so hard to be quiet. Go back to sleep. That was Cyril the butler with tea. I can save yours: it's here in a thermos. Do get some sleep, Ellie."

"Not on your life. I've had a good catnap and I need something hot in my tummy. Might as well begin this English adventure the proper way. Strong tea and strong men: I love 'em both!"

Rose laughed at her friend. "If you insist. Come over to the window, Ellie, and take the chair by the desk. I'll sit here and we can both look out while we sip. I want you to have a full view of the garden right below us. See? That's why this room is so quiet: the garden acts as a buffer for the Brompton Road racket."

"Ohhhhh," she gasped appreciatively. "Lovely. And jonquils already. Can you believe we are actually here, Rose? Wynfield Farms yesterday, London today. And to think it all started with that ratty old hairbrush of yours!"

"I had the same thought minutes ago, Ellie! I really did. But give the snow some credit. We were all feeling buried that week in February. The hairbrush gave *me* the idea but the snow got everyone else thinking. Remember those lines from Browning I quoted at our first tour meeting?

Oh, to be in England,
Now that April's there.

I was determined to be in England *this* April. Never in my wild-
est scheming did I think I'd have such a group of zany senior citizens along with me. I still wonder if I'm crazy."

"If you are, it is the craziest, most wonderful scheme you've
come up with yet. Oh, you were determined, Rose. I sensed that
from the first glimmer in your eye. You're like Max with a bone.
You don't let go until you've devoured it completely. And happily for us tagalongs, we're here to devour England *with* you!"

"Oh, I wish you hadn't mentioned Max. I know Annie was
happy to have him, but I'm going to miss that rascal something
fierce. We'll have to pick up a new leash for him at Harrods.
They carry the plaid ones. Max *does* like to look spiffy. Now,
enough talk: let's eat these scones. A Currie Street specialty.
Umm, good as ever! And gooseberry jam. I am so glad you woke
up. Tea could be saved but not the glorious scones. You're right:
I was determined to get here. And it is going to be a lark. Do you
know the first thing I'm going to do today?"

"I would not venture a guess, m'dear."

"Run over to Boots the Chemist and purchase my new hairbrush. I may even splurge and get two. Ellie, if I had not had
this trip to plan during the snow, I would have lost my mind.
Oh, isn't it heaven? Jet lag hasn't hit me yet and I think I'm
floating. You're going to be a superior roommate. I can tell by
the way you sip your tea."

"Rose, tell me something. Honestly. Do you think we'll still
be speaking after almost three weeks of togetherness?"

"Probably not. But we'll still be friends!"

They both laughed at this, spewing crumbs of scones onto the
linen napkins. Afterwards Rose and Ellie lapsed into a companionable silence. Tea grew cold in their cups as they looked down
upon a lively London waiting to be explored.

LORD NELSON
TRAFALGAR SQUARE
from ST. MARTIN IN THE FIELDS

But as the two friends enjoyed the privacy of their quiet, leaf-framed window perch and let morning tea work its wonders on tired necks and backs, their thoughts returned to Wynfield Farms and the tumult they left behind.

Rose spoke first.

"Ellie, you don't think Miss Moss would *deliberately* deceive the residents about that room, do you?"

"You mean short-change the ballot box?"

"Exactly."

"Rose, as you told me many months ago, anything is possible with 'that woman,' as poor Mary used to call her."

"Thank heavens all of us got our absentee ballots in, *and* in sealed envelopes, long before we left. Certainly could be no question about the legality of that. I wish I could forget Wynfield Farms for these next three weeks. But it's our home and just impossible to do!"

~ ~ ~

The record snowfall that paralyzed the Shenandoah Valley in February had turned out to be nature's blessing in disguise. It was soft, dry snow that, when temperatures finally moderated, melted rapidly and replenished the parched ground and filled up rivers and streams. Wynfield Farms was verdant in March, with trees bursting into new leaf and bulbs showing green above damp earth. Spring looked promising and the chill air crackled with energy.

Perhaps Spring's energies had distracted Miss Moss's attention from business duties to attention outside her well-appointed office. On one of her infrequent prowls around the kitchen and dining room area she had discovered a rather large, barren storage room. She immediately visualized it as a perfect repository for the extra filing cabinets that were encroaching on her office space, and made mental calculations of the number of such she could arrange to have moved. It was, as she described to the Wynfield Board of Directors at its March meeting, a "total waste of space except for few pantry items stored there." Unhappily for Miss Moss, she was not prepared for the Board's response to her discovery. One member, a substantial banker from Richmond, suggested that the room be renovated and turned into a public room for the residents. His suggestion was put in the form of a motion, voted upon, and the ayes carried. The only stipulation was that residents had to approve the idea of the "pub" by secret ballot with majority vote carrying. Miss Moss, an avowed teetotaler, was mortified that her discovery might soon become something as *common* as a bar where alcoholic beverages not only could be purchased but also consumed. Within the walls of Wynfield Farms. Within sight of founder Wynfield's elegant, refined dining room. Recognizing that the entire Board had started, almost instantaneously, referring to the room as "the Pub," Miss Moss had called a meeting of all residents, fully expecting that good taste would prevail and thus prevent the idea from even coming to a vote.

"I do apologize for this hastily called meeting. But the Board of Directors has requested that we make a major policy decision rather urgently and I must ask your indulgence."

Murmurs and questions crisscrossed the audience.

"It has been discovered, rather, *uncovered*, that there is a spacious closet adjacent to our beloved Wynfield dining room. So spacious, in fact, that the Board would like to authorize its renovation into a public serving room." Miss Moss's head dropped and with it, her voice. Her audience sat in silence.

"Could you repeat that Miss Moss?" came a voice from the rear of the Lounge.

"Public serving room," Miss Moss snapped. She hurled the words at the assembled.

"Are you saying a *bar* Miss Moss? The Board is willing to turn some unused closet into a bar?" This came from Father Charlie, seated as usual in the front row.

"I am indeed, Father Caldwell. Apparently one of the board members has visited other retirement communities where this is successful and wants to try it at Wynfield. Please understand it is not my idea. I am merely an instrument of the Board."

"Sounds to me like a crackerjack idea," cried Major Featherstone. "Certainly wouldn't have to worry with drunk drivers, would we? Unless wheelchairs count!" He chortled loudly at his own expense and patted his steel vehicle.

"Ellie, I swore I would never speak up again but this time I must," whispered Rose.

"Go ahead," answered Ellie. "You're the calm voice of reason here anyway."

"Miss Moss," called Rose, standing at place near the doorway. "It sounds to me as if the Board of Directors wants to change that unused room into a little pub. A cozy place to meet friends and share good talk and a bit of spirits. Now, I for one don't object to that for one minute. For heaven's sake, we are not teenagers. Wouldn't it fit the image of an Anglophile that Mr. Wynfield tried to convey in this very house? It sounds perfectly marvelous and you can count on my vote being 'Yea' right now!"

"Thank you, Mrs. McNess. Your comments will be recorded. Anyone else?"

Miss Puffenbarger spoke: "What about cost? Will it increase our monthly dues?"

"Henrietta or Harriet?" Ellie asked Rose.

"Henrietta. And she has a very important point."

"Thank you, Miss Puffenbarger. A very sound issue to raise. The Board of Directors has voted that the Wynfield Endowment Trust is sufficient to safely absorb the expenditures involved in both renovating the space and in carrying the ... public room ... for an indefinite period of time."

"That settles it for me!"

"I don't imbibe but I don't mind if my friends do so!"

"Let's tell 'em to go ahead," came another voice.

"Just one moment, please," cautioned Miss Moss. "The Board feels it must put this proposition before you, the residents, and then have a three week waiting period before the actual vote. There is the Wynfield image, after all. Some of our supporters may not approve. The final vote will be by secret ballot three weeks hence. You will receive this in the usual manner, delivered to your apartment. The ballot box will be on Miss Alexander's desk in the hall at that time. Any written comments you may wish to make may be left there at any time during the next three weeks. I will not entertain further discussion today." And *boom!* —Miss A. Elvina Moss was out of the room.

"Well, if that doesn't beat everything," shouted Bob Jenkins. "Sounds like a winner!"

Vinnie Featherstone stopped Father Charlie before he got to the door.

"Charlie, I'm anxious to hear your opinion. As a man of the cloth, do you have any serious objections?"

"Personally, no, Vinnie. I look upon it as another of Wynfield's many options. There are some here who will frequent it daily. Others may never pass through the doors. Not unlike church. But who is to say a pub is an evil thing? Not I. Nor do I think it will tarnish the Wynfield image; that is all in Miss Moss's mind. Poor sheltered soul: had a devil of a time uttering the word 'bar.' Almost as if it were going to become a den of iniquity."

"Thank you, Charlie. William and I share your opinion. She was pitiful, wasn't she? Could barely get the words out. What age does she think we've living in? Why, *speakeasies* were part of our past. Very *dim* past, you understand."

They chuckled and Father Charlie chatted further with

Vinnie as she wheeled herself slowly out the wide doors and up the hall.

Rose and Ellie remained, talking animatedly with the group clustered about them.

"I say Bravo! for the Board!" cried Frances Keynes-Livingston. "Who could possibly object to another quiet place in which to gather? Might eliminate some of our in-house parties, but not all."

Ellie wondered aloud: "I can't place what room Miss Moss was talking about. Or where, in relation to the dining room."

"Oh, this old house might have all sorts of rooms we don't know about," smiled Rose.

"Are you hinting at a mystery, Agatha?"

"No," laughed Rose, "just thinking of the many hallways and closets and cupboards that have been turned into living spaces already and wondering if they will turn up any more. Must have been some sort of a pantry, behind the mantel wall. Say, that's an idea! Maybe they'll even incorporate a fireplace into the pub. Wouldn't *that* be grand?" Her enthusiasm for the idea was contagious.

"Jolly good, Rose," chimed in Albert Warrington. "I look forward to enjoying a robust sherry there."

"If you look forward to our *faux* pub so much, Albert, have you considered joining Rose's Roamings in England the first of next month? We'll be sampling one or two public houses I'm sure!" This was the first time Rose had mentioned her proposed junket since posting her notices two days ago. Indeed, her recent bout with a raging toothache had temporarily dampened her yen for travel.

"I've been meaning to call you, Rose," spoke Frances. "Definitely count me in. Your timing could not be better. And I prefer single accommodations."

"Oh, Frances, I'm delighted," replied Rose sincerely.

"That makes three of us, Rose," cried Ellie. "We're halfway there if you only need six."

"And my meeting is Monday. Golly, sure hope I'm back to snuff by then. Oh, I will be: my tooth is all but forgotten. We can be the advance research team for the Wynfield pub. Think of all the suggestions we'll be able to bring back for the Board!"

"Will you look at the time? Rose, I don't know about you but I must change before dinner. Coming up?" This from Ellie, as the group started to disband and drift toward the doors.

"Thanks, Ellie, for keeping me on track. I'm going up, but it's tea and toast for me tonight. My jaw is still sore and I don't want to tempt fate. You know you're getting old when your teeth begin to fail. And I *feel* old right now. Besides, Max needs me. These trips to the dentist have left him alone too many times in the last few days."

When the two friends turned into their respective apartments, Rose collapsed wearily in her worn and welcoming wing chair. Unaccustomed to his mistress's languor, Max padded over and stretched out sympathetically at her feet.

"Don't worry, Max, my lethargy won't last too much longer. Give me a day or two. Remember when it snowed and I said I was having a spell of the gloomies? Well, no longer! So many things to look forward to! That's what keeps us old dogs going, isn't it? Let me sit here a minute and then I'll fix you an extra kibble. New construction, new adventures. All sorts of things around the corner. Now just where *could* that room be located? And why does the existence of a pub bother Miss Moss so much? First things first, Max; I'll get your supper. But in the morning, you and I shall investigate!"

~ ~ ~

2

"Finished, Ellie?" Rose inquired of her friend who nodded in reply. "I'll just place the tray outside the door and make it easier for Cyril's pick up. Besides, it gives us more room for unpacking. I don't know about you, but I feel wonderful. That was the right amount of food for this time of day."

"I couldn't agree more, Rose. Glad I woke up when I did. Guess what I've been thinking about these past ten minutes?"

"Wouldn't surprise me to hear you say 'Wynfield Farms.' Me, too. But we can't dwell on Wynfield, Ellie. Kate promised to fax me the results of the vote just as soon as she got them. And she'll do it. Aside from wondering about what is going on in that place, there is not one thing we can do. We're here, all of us, to enjoy England in April. Or is it April in England? And we're going to do just that. Now, what are you going to do, roomie?"

"First I'm going to hang my few things in this *very* large closet and then I'm going to take a *very* short walk. Just around the block. And then I'll probably come back up here and nap until tea time. Did you say four o'clock?"

"Four is correct. Good planning, Ellie. If you don't mind I'm going to stay here and go over notes again. I've got to finalize my proposed schedule before meeting with the guide they've assigned us. And I need to make some calls for theatre tickets."

"In other words, you'll be happy with my absence."

"Absolutely. And you know what Ellie? I'm not in the least worried that I'll offend you by saying so!"

They both laughed and in less than ten minutes Ellie finished her unpacking and slipped out the door.

Rose sat at the rosewood secretary and spread her notebook across the writing surface. She turned to the page marked PASSENGERS—April/England.

What do I really know about these people? I've known most of them not quite a year. With lifelong friends you never have to explain, or start at the beginning of a story. There is no catching up. But aside from my short hops to Poplar Forest and Monticello I've never traveled any distance with this crowd.

How would I sketch these people? That's an easy one; I wouldn't. Always did like sketching places more than people. But how would I capture such diverse personalities? The Jenkins deserve a soft-lead pencil so I could blend the outlines here and there. No color added. Yet. Father Charlie would be easy: soft pastels as in a child's portrait. He's merry and round, and except when he dons the clerical garb, a colorful character.... The Puffenbargers? I'd have to use a dun-colored crayon. With an edge. Both of them are so drab and colorless. Perhaps they'll spruce themselves up a bit over here. Get real hats, throw away the pancakes ... I'd do the remaining members with pen and ink: vigorous, decisive strokes. Certainly Ellie and Amaryllis, and absolutely Bob and Arthur. Lib ... well, I'm not too sure of her yet. She was a pretty tough cookie when Ed died. Really showed her starch.

For the time being, however, Lib is all pastel and sweetness. I'm waiting to be surprised with more than her rooming situation.

Does that really matter? Didn't I announce that Wynfield Farms was one big tour bus? And that life itself is one big tour … and that I was the leader of that tour? Well, I may eat those words. I may have bitten off more than I can handle this time.

ESTHER AND BOB JENKINS. Their enthusiasm for the trip nearly bowled Rose over. In fact, Bob Jenkins had called Rose the night her notice had appeared on the bulletin board. She knew that Bob had a good sense of humor; hadn't he named himself 'The Prowler?' But what about his aversion to walking outside? He had stated many times that he avoided going outside at any cost. "Never let your feet touch the ground, eliminate hazards, etc., etc." Was he coming to England just to please Esther? *When he realizes how much walking we'll be doing along cobblestones and rough pavement, will he still be good-natured?*

And Esther's hair. It was the texture and color of old dryer lint. Sparse and fragile, it clung to her scalp with the assistance of large, silvery old-fashioned hair-pins. Did she laugh when she set off the metal detectors at Gatwick when we came through security? She drops those pins everywhere like a trail of bread crumbs. We may have to buy her a wig in Covent Garden, poor soul.

I think the Jenkins are definitely a question mark. I'll keep special watch on them.

Rose looked at the other names on her list.

CHARLES CALDWELL. *Now that is going to be fun having Father Charlie along! Besides, how many Lambeth Conferences did he tell me he has attended? Bet he'll have a few dining recommendations for the group. And he is so congenial with everyone.*

Rose penned a large and emphatic exclamation point by Father Charlie's name.

HENRIETTA AND HARRIET PUFFENBARGER. "That dynamic duo," Rose murmured aloud. "What a pair! Octogenarian twins.

They'll probably make the London *Times* photo-op. Especially if they wear those hats!"

The Puffenbargers had hopped on every one of Rose's Roamings in the fall. Both had been enthusiastic, tireless, and curious about every door jamb and picture frame and invariably stopped to examine each monument or marker as it came into view. They were the perfect travelers: prompt, uncomplaining, dressed in sensible shoes, loose clothing, carried capacious handbags that always contained aspirin, spirits of ammonia, mints and a map of the region.

But those hats! thought Rose. Both Puffenbargers wore identical flax-colored floppy chapeaux that rested upon their heads like wilted pancakes. More curious to Rose was that the hats protected them from neither sun nor rain. Considering the twins' practical natures, this was an anomaly. The hats detracted rather than enhanced their total picture of handsomeness.

I shan't tell them, Rose decided. *I can put up with hats. I just hope they don't read every monument we encounter in London. Or Cambridge. Gosh, I've got to decide: do we try to do both Oxford and Cambridge? Or just Cambridge. Well, that is one more thing I must talk to this guide about. Depends on the crowds' wishes, I suppose, and how our time holds out.*

The Puffenbargers received a large exclamation point by their names.

ELLIE JOHNSON. *Certainly don't have any doubts about Ellie. And it will be nice to have a roommate after all these years of solitude. She knows I'll need my space every now and then. And so does she. She has such an infectious laugh: she'll keep everyone merry. Hope she doesn't tipple too much; I like my before-dinner drink but I'm not sure Ellie is willing to stop at one. But she'll be sensible.*

No, I have no doubts about Ellie Johnson.

She put a big check on the margin by Ellie's name and then glanced down the list.

FRANCES KEYNES-LIVINGSTON: The patrician *doyenne* of Wynfield Farms had mellowed considerably since her chairmanship of the first Wynfield Farms Fall Fete. Her talent with the accordion had caused her popularity to soar, and she was often asked to play for small gatherings in the Lounge. Sometimes she agreed to do so and more often, did not. There was a general understanding on the part of the residents that Mrs. Keynes-Livingston did her own thing and marched to the beat of her own drum. She had jumped into the research for her book on lichens and buried herself for days in the local libraries. When she did emerge for the public she appeared as thin as a splinter and her gray bun tumbled down her neck like a runaway tumbleweed.

She is one focused person, thought Rose. *Probably thinks she can find something on lichens of the British Isles to supplement her research. Good! We can disappear into the new library stacks together. She is one person I don't have to worry about: she'll have the underground and buses figured out by this afternoon.*

FRANCES KEYNES-LIVINGSTON. "I'm really glad she's along on this jaunt. I think she needs us as much as we need her! *Check* and double-check, Amaryllis!"

"Now that leaves who else ... let's see: Arthur Everett and Bob Lesley. And Lib Meecham. My stars, that was certainly a surprise. But they are old enough to know what they're doing, and I'm certainly not their chaperon."

Rose had been delighted when Arthur and Bob had signed up for her trip. Arthur, the ultimate intellectual, had been excited about the libraries and museums he would visit. Bob Leslie was interested in everything, from computers to gardens to antique silver. The pair had played bridge together for more than a year and was obviously comfortable in each other's company. *Perfect roommates,* Rose had decided.

Perfect they were until Lib decided to go! Or did Arthur talk her into going? She was the last to sign on. I know she felt awkward telling me about the arrangement she and Arthur had worked out. I guess that is what held her back until the last minute. Well, Charlie and Bob seemed happy enough to room together, or if they're not, they are being gentlemen about it and not whining. So that leaves Frances the only single. But she can certainly pay the single supplement easier than most, and treasures her independence. What am I fidgeting about? Looks as if everything has fallen into place just fine!

Rose put heavy check marks by the last three names: Arthur Everett, Bob Lesley, and Lib Meecham.

"Now to call those two theatres to confirm our tickets and I'll get myself unpacked. I'll wait and be surprised when the guide appears at tea time. Golly, I think I left a whole page out when I told Cyril eight for tea. We're twelve counting the guide. Thank heavens Cyril is generous with his tea goodies; adding four more won't be a problem. Here I go, talking to myself again. It's going to be a glorious trip. I just hope the guide lives up to his *advance billing.*"

~ ~ ~

PORTOBELLO ROAD

Annie dear and Jim!

London Bridge is still here! And a welcome sight. Good flight over, very smooth. Looks like I've got a grand group. Eager to meet our real GUIDE! Hugs and treats to Max, love to you both,

Mother xxx

3

By quarter past three Rose had arranged two evenings of theatre for the group, decided that they must see Oxford *and* Cambridge if only for a day's visit, unpacked her small suitcase, bathed in the generous mauve bathtub, redressed in a different skirt-and-jacket combination, and was starting out the door for her pre-tea time errands. Just as she was turning the knob Ellie burst into view down the hallway.

"Don't lock it, Rose, please! You know I would forget my key the first day!"

"Caught me just in time, Ellie. Here, it's all yours! Good timing. I'm off now to speak with Cyril and then to Boots. Don't go to sleep again, Ellie; tea at four sharp!"

"Don't worry, I'll be there. I bet I've walked ten miles. It is wonderful being in London again! I'll take a good soak and join you down there."

"You'll think you're in a purple pool; biggest bathtub I've ever seen. Felt marvelous, too!"

"Bye, then."

Rose hummed and talked to herself as she trotted down the hall.

"Eleven, including myself. A perfect size. We'll all fit into the largest van if I sit up by the driver and the guide. Wonder what kind of vehicle they've arranged for us? More important, wonder what this guide is like? Moment of truth is almost here!"

Rose cleared tea arrangements with Cyril and the kitchen staff and then headed out into the London afternoon.

"I'm not going to Boots just now; that can wait. I'm going to sit on this little bench in the sunshine and re-adjust my attitude about the guide. I've got to think positive and this is my last chance."

Rose unlatched the gate to the miniscule park in front of the Currie Street Hotel and settled herself comfortably on a corner bench. She took a thick packet of creamy vellum paper from her purse and glanced again at the first page. The navy and gold letterhead read GENERAL GUIDES in heavily embossed script. Beneath this was an imposing crest, with lions rampant. Not for the first time did Rose finger the sheets and think what handsome paper the agency used for its correspondence.

Dear Ms. McNess: We have your inquiry of 7.3 regarding the availability of a guide for your group of O.A.P. that will be convening in London 31.3 through 18/19/4. It is with the greatest of pleasure that we offer the services of an extraordinary GENERAL GUIDE who is available only because of a last-minute NATO cancellation. (This guide regularly escorts NATO families on holiday excursions.) May I assure you that Mr. David Heath-Nesbitt is the ultimate in guides. His services are superior in every way and I cannot recommend him to you more highly. For your further information I am honoured to enclose Mr. Heath-Nesbitt's CV and a few of the many testimonials we have received on his behalf. I assure you, Ms. McNess, that you will be more than satisfied with Mr. Nesbitt.

This was signed in flourishing script, "Yours most truly, Hermione L. Wainsworth."

If the flourishes were not the pinnacle of rectitude, then surely "Hermione" was.

Rose leafed through the remaining pages hastily (how many times had she read them before?) and got to the sixth page. Mr. David Heath-Nesbitt, Esq., smiled up at her in his glossy black and white 4" x 6" photo.

It's that smile, thought Rose. *He looks too confident, too debonair, too ... inexperienced. Why, he's almost smirking. Too sure of himself.*

Mr. Heath-Nesbitt wore a white shirt, sleeves rolled to the elbow, and dark trousers. Leaning casually against a British TRIUMPH, hand resting on the driver's door, the man in question did represent the prototype of British suavity.

Rose studied the photograph. *Not your usual "guide for hire" sort of photo. Decent looking fellow, I'll give him that. Certainly looks long and lanky. Who does he remind me of? That bony look ... I know! Jimmy Stewart! That's it! A British Jimmy Stewart! Well, he wasn't cocky or stuck-up. Let's hope Mr. Heath-Nesbitt is a bit like our Mr. Stewart. Wouldn't that be a rare piece of luck!*

Rose had not shared the information about the guide with anyone, not even Ellie, for fear it might be disastrous. She did not want any one of the ten to get their hopes up. If worse came to worse, she, Rose, could shepherd everyone around by herself, and GENERAL GUIDES could run and jump.

Rose smiled as she folded her papers and tucked them away in her purse. She took a deep breath and enjoyed the blue of the sky and the swaying green trees. She was glancing at her watch when a voice shattered her reverie.

"It is precisely twelve minutes before four, Madam. May I

join you on your bench for a brief rest? I promise I shall not talk."

Rose looked at this interloper who had invaded her space. Tall, graying hair, angular face with calm green eyes overhung like eaves on a house with shaggy brown eyebrows that seemed to sprout in all directions. And that voice: cultured, moderate, distinct.

Be still my heart! thought Rose in a panic. *I don't believe this is happening, but I think this is my guide.*

"I beg your pardon, sir, but *could* you be Mr. Nesbitt-Heath? A guide coming for a job...?"

"At your service, Madam. I am *indeed* Mr. David Heath-Nesbitt. And if this is the Currie Street Hotel, and this is April the first, yes, I am here to accompany a group of Americans. And you would be...?"

Rose jumped to her feet. "Rose. Rose McNess. I'm so sorry; of course it's Heath-Nesbitt. How do you do? I'm afraid I'm the one who got you into this! They are all waiting to meet you, at tea. Just about now! I hope you won't base all your impressions of Americans on my clumsiness. I was sitting here for a moment getting my thoughts together before I went in. I had no idea you'd turn up in the park. Actually, it's quite fortunate: you'll know one person before you meet the other ten. I hope I haven't scared you off."

"Scare me off? Madam, do I look the type to be easily frightened?" And then he laughed a hearty, rich rumble of a laugh that rang with sheer joy.

Rose looked at her bench companion and visibly relaxed. *What a wonderful laugh! No one who laughs like that could be seriously stuck on himself!*

"And your name, again, Madam? I'm afraid in my anxiety about the time I did not quite catch it...."

"McNess. Rose McNess. But please, call me Rose. Everyone does."

"Right-o, if I may be David, to you. I take it, Rose, you are the leader of this group?"

"Well, I am the originator of Rose's Roamings, and leader in so far as I have gotten them over here. Safely, I may add. Leader in that this was my idea, coming to London, that is. I confess I've had second thoughts about my sanity and wisdom. We are an *old* group, Mr., uh, *David*. Anything might happen."

"Ah, Rose, isn't that the beauty of it? Anything *might* happen!"

David Heath-Nesbitt was looking into Rose's eyes with a merry twinkle and a smile that was anything but a smirk. "Now, if we've got a few minutes before we beard the lion, shall we say, could you give me a run-down of your little group? Hearing the names once will prepare me for the actual introductions. And do not give *age* another thought. Here in England we celebrate and venerate age. 'Old Age Pensioner' is such a dastardly term: I prefer the 'OAPS' generation, the *mature* citizen. Of course as an OAP one does get marvelous benefits on public transports and museum tickets, all that. But you are aware of this. I'm just grateful you have no small tykes along. Now *that* situation does make me a bit uneasy."

"Any children of your own, David?"

"Oh yes, and four grands, but I'm used to them and they are well disciplined. It is the wild, untamed spoiled darling of an Ambassador that is hard to deal with on a tour. I might be taking the family through a private home and the child is determined to have his way and neither parent nor nanny curbs the behavior, and I'm supposed to give them the special spiel about ancient artifacts and authentic carpets and no one is listening ... I say, I am *sorry*! Here I am prattling on when we have precious minutes left before our meeting. The names, Rose, can you run them by me?"

"Better than that, David. Here is the group, consigned to paper, with a thumbnail description of each, *and* their room number in the Currie Street. It is a mixed bag, but a fairly jolly group, or at least I hope so. *And* healthy. Yes, so far everyone is healthy."

"'No walkers nor chairs, then?"

"No. But I have urged the twins to carry a cane. And Bob Jenkins. You'll see the members' idiosyncrasies jotted beside each name. And their home state."

"Something tells me you've put more than a little effort into the planning of this trip, Rose. Believe me, that pre-trip effort pays off. Brilliant! Now, what say we go in for tea? I suddenly have a beastly hunger for food and new friends. Shall we?"

"David, since it is precisely three minutes before tea time, I say let's go!"

For the first time, I feel absolutely certain that I have done the right thing in coming to England. Why then, thought Rose, allowing David Heath-Nesbitt to take her elbow as they crossed the street to the Currie, *are my cheeks flushed and my heart beating wildly?*

~ ~ ~

4

"Thank you, Cyril," smiled Rose, acknowledging the fourth tray of sandwiches and pastries that the wizened butler had placed upon the wide table. "I think we have everything we need. It looks perfect. And even fresh flowers! I'll ring when we're through. It may not be for quite a while."

"Yes, Madam," wheezed the ancient attendant, bowing his way shakily from the private lounge.

Bless Cyril, thought Rose. *I suspect he's been here since they opened the doors of the Currie Street. Did he leave us any milk for our tea? Of course, there it is.*

"Welcome, everyone! Yoo hoo … welcome!" Rose tried the second time to make her voice heard above the din of excited voices that seemed to escalate with each passing minute.

"Ladies, gentlemen. There is someone I want you to meet. Rose tapped a spoon against a water goblet and effected the *ding-ding-ding* of a cheap bell. "Ladies, gentlemen, we are here at last. And it is my great pleasure to introduce you to our guide, and our friend, Mr. David Heath-Nesbitt. Mr. Heath-Nesbitt will be with us every step of the way during our stay in his city. Mr. Heath-Nesbitt, would you care to say a few words?"

"Wynfielders all," the guide boomed. "I am delighted to see each of you and shall endeavor to learn your name as I introduce myself to you in just a moment. But first let me say, I am *David*. I become Mr. Heath-Nesbitt when purchasing tickets or confronting the constabulary, but for everyday use, please, call me David. Second, I am raging with hunger and should like to tuck into this splendid Currie Street tea and I have a notion that most of you would, also. Let me suggest that we fortify ourselves with food and drink and then Rose and I shall lay out our plans for the fortnight."

"Hear, hear!" shouted Father Charlie. "A man after my own heart!"

Hungry travelers eagerly snatched up sandwiches and savories and sipped the strong, hot brew that Rose kept refilled in their cups. Each person had a personal story of falling asleep on foreign soil or some curious piece of trivia about his or her room. Clearly, each member of the group exuded good cheer, good health, and a generous feeling of self-pride for having made it across the Atlantic without senescence crimping their style.

"Rose," whispered Harriet Puffenbarger as she nibbled her egg salad sandwich, "let me tell you about our lavatory. We have a mahogany throne on a raised dais! With an Oriental rug covering the entire room. You simply must come see it, Rose. Sister is going to take a picture."

Rose giggled between bites of her own sandwich. "I'm sure they gave that room to you two because they suspected you were visiting royalty. The *dais* is reserved for honored guests or visiting heads of state. You and Henrietta probably have the only one in the hotel. Didn't I tell you the Currie Street was full of curious little touches like that? It's Old World."

"Oh, you warned us, Rose," chimed in Frances Keynes-

Livingston. "I think you neglected to tell us about the lifts. I noted that they had been inspected but they certainly would not pass any speed test. But the Currie *is* charming and I for one have no complaints."

"And you, Esther: how is your room?" asked Rose timorously. Of all the guests, she wanted the Jenkins to be completely satisfied.

"Perfect, my dear. Bob Jenkins hit that bed as soon as we got our luggage and never moved for three hours. He's never slept as soundly. Why, he hasn't even unpacked. Nor looked at the view. I think we can see St. Paul's from our window."

"Maybe not St. Paul's, Esther, but perhaps similar architecture. But your room *is* nice?"

"Rose, it is charming. All in shades of blue, with a tea kettle in the corner and a decanter of sherry. Of course we didn't have a drop before we came down."

"But it's there for you, Esther, any time you wish. And don't hold Bob back!" Charlie Caldwell had joined in this good natured banter and was enjoying the Jenkins' pleasure as much as Rose.

Ellie sidled up to Rose. She balanced her tea cup in one hand and a dainty *petit four* in the other. "Rose you rascal! Why didn't you tell me about this divine guide?"

"Shhhh, Ellie. I didn't know. Honestly! He *is* rather distinguished, don't you think? Wait, I think he's about to say something to the group." She waved her friend to be silent.

David Heath-Nesbitt, having introduced himself to each of the tour members, and eaten more than an ample quantity of sandwiches and cakes and candied fruits, stood in front of the tea table and raised his hand.

"If I may, please, have your attention? Please find a comfy seat and I shall get on with formalities. Please help yourself to more tea before sitting. Now, I shall try to keep my part of this program brief. And informal. Please ask questions if they pop into your mind. I shall try to answer everything you may throw at me. And remember, *no* question is silly."

They all found seats and visibly relaxed, waiting for the oracle to speak.

"For the fortnight of your holiday here in London, this shall be our launching pad. We shall gather at 0900 *sharp* each morning and return no later than 1800 in the evening. Unless, of course, there are alternate plans. Any problem with those hours?"

"About 1800," came Henrietta's voice, "is that five in the evening?"

"Sorry, didn't mean to confuse you, madam. No, that is *six* o'clock. So glad you asked."

Nods and cheerful smiles greeted this exchange.

"I realize that many of you have different interests here in London and that you may not desire to accompany the group on any or every daily excursion. Perfectly fine. Please, just notify your roommate or Rose of your plans. The Bobbies here do a fine job of rounding up vagrants but we don't want them collecting lost tourists. In a few moments we shall make a rapid swing around a few major highlights. I like to call this my 'London by Twilight' tour. Tomorrow morning we shall retrace our steps and visit both the Parliament buildings and Westminster, *and* the Cabinet War Rooms if time allows. One of my favorites. You'll almost vow you can smell the cordite and hear the buzz bombs down there. You'll learn that I do have my favorite spots as we wheel around this city. I like to stop promptly at half-twelve for lunch, usually at a pub or one of the museums in our touring vicinity. And of course we do have our tea stop written in for four each day."

Bob Jenkins interrupted Mr. Heath-Nesbitt at this point by a clap of his hands and exclaiming, "Right on! We can do some serious research on public rooms!"

The crowd burst into laughter and voiced their agreement. Rose saw that their guide was bewildered. His expression was one of puzzlement and his shaggy eyebrows were raised in surprise.

"David, if I may? Our retirement home, Wynfield Farms, is adding a pub to the premises and we thought we could do some research while on our trip. Call us the 'advance scouting party'."

"Wynfield Farms is *voting* to add a pub, Rose. Not a foregone conclusion by any means. We should find out in a week or so." Bob Lesley spoke forcefully. He was one of the pub's more staunch—and vocal—supporters.

"I thought I told all of you that Kate Alexander is going to fax me just as soon as the vote is announced. I expect we'll hear within the week," said Rose. "Sorry for the interruption, David, but we're a little nervous about what's going on back home. Please, continue."

"Perfectly understandable. I'll be eager to hear myself what decision you reach. Let me see, where was I? Oh. We shall, of course, take in all of the major museums and galleries: The National, Tate, Wallace, British Museum, and day after tomorrow, the V&A. For those of you unfamiliar with the *grande dame* of British museums, that is the beloved Victoria and Albert, right up here on Cromwell. I have taken the liberty of printing up the schedule for our daily trips but before I pass them out I want you to know that changes can and shall be made. Always happens. Now, any questions so far?"

"David, how will we be getting about in London?"

"Thank you, Arthur. It is Arthur, am I correct?"

"*Veritas!*"

"*Quomodo vales?*" shot back David Heath-Nesbitt.

Oh no, gasped Rose, *I forgot he studied the classics at Oxford. Two of them now!*

"Good question, my friend. We shall be using public trans-

portation when feasible. Do all of us good to use our OAP card
and to move about, experience the underground and buses. For
longer trips the van shall be at the ready. We have at our disposal
a customized Hummer wagon, capable of holding twelve per-
sons plus the driver, and any luggage those twelve might have. I
assure you that losing sight of this vehicle is nigh impossible. But
I'll say no more. I look forward to introducing you to it, *and* our
marvelous driver, Mr. Peter Bolt. As soon as this session is over
we shall embark on our first rideabout. Rose, may I ask you to
pick up the discussion at this point? I am sure there are arrangements you would like to discuss."

"Thank you, David. Actually, you have covered just about
everything. Except dinners and the theatre. Tonight is my treat.
We are all dining in the Currie Street: main dining room at
seven-thirty. I hope that will give everyone enough time after our
twilight tour. You realize, I am sure, that you have vouchers for
eight more dinners here at the Currie. All you need do is fill out
the tag and leave it on your bedroom door *in the morning*. That
assures you a place at the table that evening. If your plans
change, the Currie does not charge you and your voucher is
good the next evening. Or the next. I am going to supplement
David's handout with one of my own: a list of nearby restaurants
that I can personally recommend. Oh, I confirmed our theatre
tickets this afternoon. Next Thursday the Royal Shakespeare
Company performing "Much Ado" at the Barbican and Tuesday
before we leave, a new musical at the Majesty. Dinner those
nights will be *after* the theatre: the only proper thing to do."

"May I suggest your friends have an ample tea on those days,
Rose?"

"I'm ahead of you, David. I've booked tea at Brown's before
the Shakespeare and Claridge's for the last."

"We are living 'high on the hog' as they say in Virginia, Rose,"
called Father Charlie.

LONDON COLISEUM
(from the UPPER LOUNGE)

"Aren't we just?" murmured Lib Meecham, seated cozily beside Arthur Everett.

A *double entendre*? wondered Rose, glancing in the direction of her friend Lib. "We did come over here to enjoy ourselves, didn't we? I would suggest that our philosophy during the next three weeks be one of complete solipsism: the self is the only reality. And our selves crave enjoyment." With that tidbit Rose nodded to David Heath-Nesbitt and sat down.

"Bravo, Mrs. Rose McNess," asserted the guide. "I applaud both your spirit and your philosophy. I shall be here to prevent anyone becoming a sybarite, however!"

"*Touché*, David," smiled Rose.

"Now, without further ado, may I escort you to our waiting coach? I shall stand at the door and personally place our schedules in your hand as you exit. The gentleman at the Hummer, our driver *extraordinaire* Mr. Peter Bolt, will help you to your seat. This way, please."

The crowd came to life, gathering up jackets and sweaters and enthusiasm simultaneously and lining up patiently for the handouts and one more word with the popular David.

Whew! Rose sighed, *that is over. What a grand crowd! No complainers, no whiners, no one unhappy with their room. And David: what a hit! I don't believe our luck.*

Rose signaled to a hovering Cyril that the group was finished and then walked slowly toward the Currie's main entrance doors. Before her, parked exactly in front on the hotel's wide apron, was the strangest, brightest yellow vehicle Rose had ever seen.

"Your coach awaits, Madam," announced David Heath-Nesbitt, bowing from the waist and winking one calm green eye at Rose. "The Hummer is at your service!"

~ ~ ~

5

"What do you think? Does GENERAL GUIDES' lorry meet your expectations?"

Rose stared. And stared again. The massive vehicle was rooted to the London pavement on four bulky, solid tires. With box-like appearance and square windows it resembled no automobile or truck that Rose had ever seen. It was almost as high as it was long, the double-decker section, as David explained, "customized for the company." "GENERAL GUIDES," distinctive in navy and gold script, flowed across both front doors. Underneath this discreet personalization was the crest that Rose recalled from Hermione's letterhead.

"Does it meet your approval, Rose?" questioned a now-anxious Mr. Heath-Nesbitt. "Your friends seem to have taken to it."

"Our own private double-decker," squealed Ellie, already seated in the second row. "Plenty of room for all of us, Rose. Come on, get in."

"I think it is marvelous, David. I don't know what I was expecting but this is ... out of this world. A cheese box on wheels! There cannot be another like this in London. Or all of the British Isles for that matter! And bright as a canary. Wynfield's own canary!"

"Actually, it's called 'competition yellow,' but canary it shall be. And can this budgie fly! Here, let me introduce you to Peter Bolt."

Peter Bolt was built along the same lines of the Hummer: square, solid, rooted to the ground. He swept off his dashing dark blue cap and bowed to Rose as David introduced them.

"And will we be off now, sir?" he asked David.

"As soon as Mrs. McNess finds a seat. I'll ride up with you as usual and identify the landmarks. Where would you like to sit, Rose? Up here with us or in the rear?"

"'E's both comfy, we can say that, can't we Mr. David?"

"Assuredly, Peter. Genuine leather seats, too; our Hummer has everything."

"I believe I'll sit in the rear, David. That way I can lean back and relax. This tour belongs to you and Peter now." She climbed in the open door and slid in beside Bob Lesley. Which meant pushing Lib and Arthur closer together toward the far side but Rose noticed they did not seem to mind this one bit.

"And we're off, ladies and gentlemen! Again, welcome to London. This shall be a very quick overall glimpse of some of my city's monuments. As you can see, it is barely five o'clock and the light is fading rapidly. But in your next two weeks you'll notice there will be a gradual increase of daylight each day. If you stayed until June you could read the *Times* outside at ten in the evening. We shall be driving down Chelsea Embankment towards Victoria, keeping the mighty Thames to your right as we travel. No, no, that is not London Bridge yet, nor Tower Bridge. I'll tell you when they come into sight. Fairly soon you'll catch sight of Westminster Abbey and Big Ben, and the Houses of Parliament. Yes, right over there...."

David's enthusiasm was genuine and contagious. Heads turned and fingers pointed as the group barreled along under Peter's steady driving.

Rose rested her head against the sleek cushion and looked around at her companions. She had deliberately chosen the rear seat in order to observe her fellow passengers.

Charlie Caldwell was seated behind David Heath-Nesbitt, and they leaned toward each other in animated conversation. *Those two will enjoy one another. Why, I bet they will have a pub date before we get back to the Currie. David. I better try and stick to Mr. Heath-Nesbitt regardless. I wonder what he thinks of Rose's Roamings?*

Esther and Bob Jenkins were seated beside Charlie and behind the driver. Rose could see Esther's head turning first to the window and then back to Bob, then to the window and back to Bob. *Regular as a windshield wiper.* Rose smiled. *They are really going to enjoy themselves. I can tell already. Oh, dear God, don't let Bob Jenkins trip on a cobblestone and end up in plaster. Give me my faith in double doses, Lord, and let me keep Bob within my field of vision whenever possible. But hey! We are mature, senior citizens. I better keep reminding myself of that. I volunteered to lead this group, not hold their hands.* Rose could not help but smile as she continued to watch the Jenkins' enjoyment. Peter Bolt was now contributing to the conversation as he pointed out the sights.

"Right you are, ladies and gents: St. Paul's it is. Dome number two *only* to St. Peter's in Rome, but we can grant the Holy Father that 'un! But Great Paul, the very bell in the south tower, is over seventeen tons. Don't think even the Holy Father can boast that!"

"And is it the original St. Paul's, Mr. Bolt?"

"This 'er's Sir Christopher Wren's St. Paul's, which he built to replace the old St. Paul's what tumbled in the Great Fire. Only St. Paul's I know, so it's original to me!"

Gracious! A classicist guide and a driver who is up on his architecture and tonnages. We'll be saturated with facts when we return home.

Both the Puffenbargers had opted for the upper level of the Hummer, slowly climbing the winding metal ladder, and now reveling in their views. Frances had joined them and Rose could hear shrieks of hilarity from this unlikely trio. *Such curious, dear ladies. The Puffenbargers are going to love London and London will love them back. And Frances is having the most fun she's had in years.*

"Tired, Rose?" asked Bob Lesley with honest solicitation.

Rose thought for the umpteenth time how fortunate it was that Bob was on the trip.

"I'd be less than truthful if I said 'no,' Doctor. But nothing that a good meal and a real night's sleep won't dismiss. Aren't we lucky with the weather … so far?"

"Ah, yes, Rose. I just keep reminding myself that this is an island and it is April, so things may change in the wink of an eye. Great to be here, isn't it?"

"Bob now *your* solipsism is showing!" laughed Rose. "I'm glad you decided to come. You'll add so much. And I'm sure you know a lot more history about these places than I do."

"Pssh, Rose. Nothing escapes you. That is precisely why we all feel like we are literally in your hands. Safe and secure with Rose's Roamings."

"And now, thank heavens, with GENERAL GUIDES and Mr. Heath-Nesbitt. I can relax, Bob. I think our Mr. Heath-Nesbitt is going to be a fine guide."

"Surely appears that way to me after our initial meeting. You two will be quite a team. Now, I'll shut up so we can listen to what our guide is saying."

Rose caught the words "Fleet Street" and realized how far the Hummer had traveled from Currie Street. She glanced to her right and saw Lib and Arthur gesturing toward some placard. Could they have spotted part of the old Roman wall?

I hope Arthur Everett knows what he is doing. What a surprise that was, his asking me if I had any objections to his rooming with Lib. What could I say? Why not Lib? She would not have come on this trip without a roommate. She couldn't have afforded the single supplement. Still, as pleasant and competent as Lib Meecham is, she's bound to be more complicated beneath her cool, impersonal librarian's demeanor. But Arthur seems so happy with her. Does he want more than a roommate? Does he want the encumbrances I suspect this arrangement brings with it? Rose, that is none of your business. Keep repeating that: none of your business. We are senior adults.

If Rose had been privy to the conversation between Lib Meecham and Arthur Everett prior to their signing for her tour she might have had fewer misgivings about the "arrangement."

~ ~ ~

After finishing two quick hands of bridge with the Cunninghams, Lib and Arthur strolled back to Lib's apartment.

"Come in, Arthur. We must talk," said Lib.

"Absolutely, Lib. I confess I've been avoiding this. The talking, that is."

"Sit down and make yourself comfortable, Arthur." Lib sat in the chair opposite his.

"Do you really want to go through with this: taking me on as a roommate? We must let Rose know something definite by tomorrow."

"Lib, as I told you before: this presents no problem to me.

None whatsoever. I am not the world's most exciting widower, nor am I the most dangerous. I want to travel, and travel by the most economical means. This is too good a trip to let slip away. Having a roommate with whom to share expenses makes it all the more attractive. I'm not even going to discuss it with my children. If sharing a room with a member of the opposite sex bothers *you*, please speak freely, dear Lib."

"It does not bother me," assured Lib shyly. "It is ever so much nicer to come in after a full day and talk and share experiences with someone you enjoy. Rather than returning to an empty, cold room or even collaring another fellow traveler in the lounge. But let me make one thing clear. I will not cling like a leech and I certainly will not make demands on you as a roommate. Just give me my share of the closet and bureau and I shall be content. Agreed?"

"Absolutely. I regard you with the utmost respect and value your advice and wisdom. It is my considered opinion that you will be a perfect traveling companion. And with your knowledge of the Bard, think of the literary adventures we shall share."

~ ~ ~

At six-thirty the Wynfield Canary pulled up in front of the Currie Street Hotel and Peter Bolt jumped from his seat to assist his passengers.

"Peter, that was the best London-by-twilight tour I've ever had. Beats any bus or train for speed and comfort." Rose moved to shake Peter's hand as she complimented his driving. "Fate has smiled on us in sending you to be our driver."

"Ow, Missus. Know this city like the back of m'hand. Nothin' to it. Ye've got a rare group 'ere. Int'rested in ev'rthing. Leave it to Mr. David and old Peter: we'll show 'em the sights." Peter Bolt's ruddy cheeks grew ruddier with each word.

"You've started off on the right foot, Peter. I want you to keep spoiling us. We'll look forward to seeing you in the morning."

"Rose, a word, please." Mr. Heath-Nesbitt turned from escorting Frances and the twins into the Currie. "I hope we didn't ramble too far this first outing. For their first day, it may have been a bit much. We did cover more than I had planned. But they all seemed enthusiastic."

"It was wonderful. Didn't see anyone dozing, did you? But I guarantee we'll sleep tonight."

"First rate. I'm impressed with your friends. A lively group! Not your usual pensioners. One thing we didn't discuss today, however. You mentioned in your letter to Hermione that you wanted to see Oxford or Cambridge. Have you made any decision as to which?"

"Not really,... David. I'm going to rely on your good judgment. But could we postpone that decision until tomorrow? I really am starting to wilt and I have yet to find a post box."

"Oh, I say, how thoughtless of me. Of course you must be tired. Here, let me post your letters. There is one opposite my flat. It will go out tonight."

"Just a couple of cards, really, but I'd appreciate that. Have to keep in touch with the family at home. Thanks, David. And now, I'm off to freshen up and rest a minute before dinner. Shall we say until 0900 in the morning?"

"Righto!" he called, and was off in the Hummer with Peter Bolt.

~ ~ ~

THE CURRIE STREET HOTEL
Founded 1899

London

Dear Kate!

How I wish you were with us! A fun group of travelers and easy to be with. So much to tell, from sights, theatre, funny incidents.

You won't believe all that we've done so far. Our guide is just wonderful (DAVID). Keep the home fires burning until we return!

Love,

Rose McN.

THE CURRIE STREET HOTEL
Founded 1899

London

April

Dear Susan! (And all the Wordsworth gals!)
How you'd love England in April! Sorry to
miss the Lake District this trip but there are
daffodils simply everywhere! Bet they are
blooming at home, too! And there's another
flower show to put on your calendar:
Sandringham's. First started in 1881. Maybe
next year?

　　　Love to you and all the members,

　　　　　　　Rose

(Postcard to Mrs. Susan Warfield of Wynfield Farms)

6

CARITAS · PRIVILEGIO · HABET

Kate Alexander was a picture of abject depression. She looked at the calendar spread before her and sighed. The Wynfield Farms' Reception Hall was an empty cavern at half-past eight this Tuesday morning. The attractive redhead propped her elbows on the desk and rested her chin further between her hands.

Why don't I hear something from Tom Brewster? How could any man be so heartless? Three months and one postcard. I know he's proud and stubborn but really, this is absurd. And now with Mrs. McNess away, I don't have anyone I can talk to. A mistake, that's what it was, letting myself fall for him. Tom probably thinks he can love 'em and leave 'em. Just discard women like an old pair of loafers. Well, I'll show him. I'm going to make my own plans. Tom Brewster can call Wynfield Farms after June 6 and find Kate Alexander gone!

Morose as she was, Kate Alexander realized she had just jumped two squares in life's game of checkers. She would receive her Master of Arts degree in mid-May. Already she had responded to several job interviews in the Roanoke Valley. Neither had enticed her. An interesting situation in Raleigh still piqued her interest. She had yet to answer the Director's letter regarding that one. *Yes, the time has come for me to get on with my life. And not wait for any man.*

If I worked here at Wynfield until the middle of May, that would give me plenty of time for a short break, packing, and then time to resettle in Raleigh. I know I can get that job: this is the second letter I've had from the director. I'll answer today and see if I can wangle an interview for early next week. If I focus on my future I won't have time to think about the what ifs. Especially what if with Tom Brewster. Isn't that what Mrs. McNess would tell me to do? Crowd out the unpleasant with the pleasant and look ahead with hope? But I was so hopeful about Tom!

At this thought of the insoluble, Kate gave in to deepest melancholy and put her head down on her arms. She sobbed quietly, wet tears causing the ink to blur the April calendar with slow, blue rivers that puddled and then ran some more. She did not hear approaching footsteps.

"What's this? A pity party? Miss Alexander, no man is worthy of your tears!"

"Mr. Warrington." Kate jumped in her embarrassment, wiping both eyes hastily. "I'm so sorry you found me like this. Really. I'll be all right. It's nothing ... really."

"Next you'll be telling me it's allergies. You look dreadful, Miss Alexander. Here, take my handkerchief. No, better still. You retreat to the Ladies' Room and I shall stay here and man the telephone. Cannot leave the place unattended."

Kate was mortified by her discomfort and more so by being discovered by Albert Warrington. The meek, mild-mannered bachelor had gained fame, even notoriety, as the Yale taxidermist after his confession at the famous Wynfield Fall Fete. And now he, the confirmed bachelor, was diagnosing *her* love life. Kate had a wild impulse to giggle, but if she did....

"Thank you, Mr. Warrington. I'll do just that. Back in a sec." And she made a rapid retreat to the Ladies' Room off the hall.

Albert Warrington positioned his briefcase beside the desk, unbuttoned his anorak, and settled into Kate's chair. Two minutes later Miss Moss emerged from her office. Startled at his presence, she strode purposely toward him.

"Good morning, Mr. Warrington," Miss Moss enunciated in well-modulated tones. "And may I inquire as to the nature of your disposition this morning?"

"My disposition is fine, Miss Moss, just fine. Both internal and external. Miss Alexander had a sudden sneezing fit as I was passing by and I told her I would man the desk until she readjusted her contact lenses. Why, here she comes now. I'll happily relinquish my post. Good morning to you both. Sneezing all over, Miss Alexander?"

"Snee ... *yes*! Yes, Mr. Warrington, thank you so much. I feel much better now." Kate had rinsed the red from her eyes and once more appeared radiant.

"Allergies, Miss Alexander, allergies. Best take drastic steps now rather than worry with them all your life." He smiled knowingly at Kate, nodded to both women and walked briskly to the door.

"A singular individual," murmured Miss Moss.

"A wonderful man. A real gentleman. And full of wisdom," sighed Kate, realizing again what her next step should be. As soon as Miss Moss left she would put in that call to Raleigh and arrange an interview. Sooner rather than later.

"You do realize, Miss Alexander, that today is the day I count the votes."

"I certainly do, Miss Moss. They have been coming in right and left. And of course Mrs. McNess's tour put their votes in before they left. Every single one of them."

"*They would.* Ah, Miss Alexander, you are far too young to comprehend. Some things do not need changing. I fear the inclusion of a public room at Wynfield would upset the entire meal system we have so carefully regulated. Our residents are accustomed to the routines and the hours...."

"But if the public room is favorably voted upon, and that might be a bigger *if* than we both think, wouldn't it be optional for the residents? I mean, no one is forcing anyone to go into the public room. Each to his own taste, hasn't that been the motto here more or less?" Kate looked at Miss Moss with innocent curiosity.

"You know how these folks are, Miss Alexander," continued Miss Moss. "Various states of senility. They follow like sheep. Where one goes, the others follow. A public room will disrupt napping, dining, planned outings, as well as encourage alcoholism, lethargy and...."

Kate did not allow the Director of Residence to continue her condescending litany. She stood and asked, "Miss Moss, may I interrupt?"

Startled, Miss Moss looked at the young receptionist and said abruptly: "Certainly."

"Miss Moss, I have been working here at Wynfield Farms for the past two years. I have come to know and love many of the residents. *I can't say how much I love one of their grandsons!* I also have been getting my Masters in Sociology during those two years. Now, both experiences, my studies and my on-the-job training, convince me that not one person here in Wynfield Farms is so weak that he or she will be led astray by the construction of one small bar. Furthermore, I am convinced that the room will encourage more group gatherings, more merriment, more enjoyment of evenings that can be long and lonely. Think of the average age here, Miss Moss. Hardly a bunch of teenagers."

"Miss Alexander, you are paid for your responsibilities as Hostess and Receptionist, not as a director of social policies. Obviously your mind is made up. Well, so is mine, and neither of us has a vote on the issue. We shall see how the residents view this intrusion. The Board is arriving at two this afternoon and votes shall be counted at the meeting. Now, I must be...."

"One more thing, Miss Moss," cried Kate, rising in place. "I shall be submitting my resignation to the Board today. In writing, of course. But I wanted to let you know first. Before the written letter."

Done! thought Kate. *There, I've said it! No retraction now!*

"Miss Alexander, that is preposterous. Because you and I happen to differ on one or two matters! Resigning is not the solution, my child."

My child?

"Oh, no, Miss Moss. Our differences have nothing to do with my resignation." *Well, not exactly honest but I can fudge to keep the peace.* "I have been looking for a position closer to my home. In North Carolina. Since I finish my degree in May, it is time I gave notice."

"I don't know what to say, Miss Alexander. You've been ... an asset to our home. I never dreamed that you would leave. You have considered this from all angles, I presume?"

"Oh, yes, Miss Moss. I've had time to think it all over, as well as look into other opportunities. I'll have the letter on your desk by noon."

Miss Moss shook her head slowly as if she had not yet taken in the full import of Kate Alexander's words. She turned and walked wearily back to her office.

Whew, surmised Kate. *I'm glad she brought up the pub issue. That just ticked me off. I had no idea I was going to blurt out my intentions. Not this early, anyway. It just came out! But it is just six weeks from today. I sure do miss Rose McNess, even more than Tom right now. I need someone I can talk to!*

Kate shrugged and pulled out her pen. She began drafting her letter of resignation from the best job she had ever held.

~ ~ ~

7

THE CURRIE STREET HOTEL
Founded 1899

"Mrs. McNess! Delighted to see you once again!" The tall, distinguished gentleman immaculate in navy pinstripe suit rushed forward to greet Rose as she and Ellie walked up the three entry steps to the Currie Street lobby. Hand extended, he bent his head slightly, and brushed Rose's left cheek, then her right. Rose registered mentally that his mustache smelled faintly of a familiar heady scent she had purchased at Liberty's long ago for her husband. *But which husband?*

"The Currie Street Hotel welcomes you, Mrs. McNess, and this marvelous entourage you have brought with you. So sorry I was away at conference for the past three days. I trust my staff has seen to your every comfort?" He bowed slightly at his rhetorical question.

"Mr. Harley! You are, as we Americans say, a sight for sore, tired eyes. Come, please, let me introduce you to my friend and roommate, Ellie Johnson. Ellie, my friend Mr. Randolph

Paul Harley, Esquire, Manager of the last, small independent hotel in London. For how many years now, Mr. Harley?"

"Let us not reveal all of our secrets, Mrs. McNess. Let us just say that I have been manager here as long as you have graced us with your presence while in London. And you, Mrs. Johnson, are from…?" Again he bowed low, still holding Ellie's extended hand.

"Virginia, Mr. Harley. Wynfield Farms. Rose and I are residents there as well as good friends. This is our first tour as roommates, however!"

"Charmed, Mrs. Johnson. A pleasure to welcome you to the Currie Street."

"He's quite the diplomat, Ellie, as if I needed to tell you that. Your staff, and especially dear old Cyril, has been wonderful. We've dined here the past three nights and I don't think I can persuade any of my group to go elsewhere. They rave about the gourmet food and accuse the waiters of holding Elizabeth David hostage in the kitchen. Of course, I think most of the help is too young to even appreciate Elizabeth David, but the older ones smile appreciatively. And the veal last night … oh my, it was particularly succulent, Mr. Harley."

"Perhaps your friends will enjoy the words of a Reverend Sidney Smith:

>Serenely full, the epicure would say,
>Fate cannot harm me,
>I have dined today."

"I love that," cried Ellie. 'Fate cannot harm me, I have dined today.' Think that'll hold during our stay here, Rose?"

"I hope," agreed Rose.

"And your rooms, Mrs. McNess? Satisfactory?"

"I can answer that, Mr. Harley," chimed in Ellie. "Elegant. Never hear a sound at night and wake up to Cyril's bountiful tea trays in the morning. Perfect, wouldn't you say, Rose?"

"That is precisely what we strive for, Mrs. Johnson: elegant surroundings and old fashioned courtesy. We want the Currie Street to become your 'home away from home.' And now if you ladies will excuse me, I must run and consult with Chef. Formal dinner this evening in the Peacock Room. May I count on seeing you both later?" Again the bow from the waist.

"He's a smooth one, Rose," Ellie whispered as soon as Mr. Harley was out of earshot. "Certainly makes a dandy impression. Think he dyes that head of black hair?"

"I'm sure of it," replied Rose. "I've been coming here for over twenty years and he's never aged one iota. Never seen him in anything but a three-piece pinstripe suit, either. Navy blue or black. Goes with the image of the bank manager or hotel manager, doesn't it?"

"I was thinking that he and Miss Moss would be a good pair. I think pinstripe suits are the only thing in *her* wardrobe, too."

"Ellie, you're terrible." Rose pushed the lift button to the fifth floor and the pair waited for the ancient contraption to jolt to a halt before them.

"After you, Rose," said Ellie, holding the gate. "I still have enough strength to do this even after the morning at Harrods."

"That was a good idea of David's, don't you think, giving us until two this afternoon to shop or just look around? And he said we'd do that about every third day. Keeps interest in the museums and galleries at top level when we return to the business of sightseeing."

By this time they had reached their floor and were walking down the carpeted corridor.

"What other good ideas does David have in store for us, Rose?" sassed Ellie.

"Ellie, don't you start! I can tell you are just itching to question me. David Heath-Nesbitt is a fine guide with excellent instincts. I think he has our best interests at heart."

"If you ask me, Rose, you chose Mr. Heath-Nesbitt for his looks and *coincidentally* found a great guide in the bargain. As the Brits say, 'David is smashing.' I wouldn't care if he couldn't lead us out of a paper bag. I'd follow him on looks alone."

"Ellie, you are ridiculous. I took what GENERAL GUIDES sent me. All I had to go on before we met was the resume the firm sent me. He certainly is overqualified for this job, though. Classics degree from Jesus College in Oxford, advanced degree from London School of Economics, more studies in Germany. He was a perpetual student. But he's been at this guide work for the past twenty-five years so he must love his chosen profession."

"Right now he loves his profession of squiring you around, Rose. I can see it when he looks at you. Why, I bet he'd love to give you a private English history lesson starting at 1066 and coming on up to present times. I foresee ... romance for Rose!" Ellie guffawed and threw herself on her bed.

"Ridiculous, I say, Ellie. You are being plain ridiculous. And he doesn't look at me in any special way," Rose decried.

"If you'd stop being so bristly and defensive and let yourself have a chance, you might find you'd enjoy the romance in this!" With this last, Ellie bounced off the bed and stood, arms akimbo, facing her friend.

"I admit I was a little shaken that first day. He is awfully attractive. And I was expecting someone years younger. GENERAL GUIDES is too smart to put their guides' ages down in print; David is nearly our age. He's 69. A pensioner himself."

"A younger man. Bravo! Go for a younger man, Rose, you've already buried two husbands. If romance should flare, I shall fan the flames. Myself, I rather like Peter Bolt. 'Fancy him,' as the shopgirls say."

"Enough of this, Ellie. My life is full to overflowing right now. What do I need with a man in my life? Temporarily or permanently. I've been so lucky and so happy twice before—knock wood! —I'm not about to take any more chances."

"Oh all right. No use trying to change *your* mind. I know you too well for that. Just promise me, Rose, that you'll enjoy his company while you've got it? He's such a classy gent! And if the truth be told, I'm a little envious of you," Ellie added wistfully.

"Thank you, Ellie. I do appreciate your invaluable concern. And advice. Now, enough of this talk. It isn't too late for me to shuttle you off to Frances Amaryllis. I'll tell her that I need more time for planning and you are being disruptive."

"And then you could sneak David Heath-Nesbitt in for an after-hours *private* history lesson. What do the French call it: *cinq à sept*? Ah, Rose, you are getting downright devious in your Medicare years."

"Ellie, stop this silliness and let me pour you a cuppa. We have one half-hour before we join the others and walk up to the Victoria and Albert Museum. And I'll insist that you walk up front with David. That is, if you promise not to bend *his* ear with any of your twaddle."

"I promise, Rose. You know I'm teasing. Except for what I said about enjoying his company while you've got it: I mean that! Changing the subject, did you ever get that new hairbrush you came over here to buy?"

"I did, Ellie, thank you very much. In fact, I splurged and bought *two* while I was at it."

Rose poured boiling water from the automatic tea kettle on the corner table and watched the tea grow dark and steamy. She did not look at Ellie as she removed the tea bags and handed her friend a cup. Never, never would she admit to Ellie, much less to herself, that there might be an inkling of truth in her roommate's jesting.

~ ~ ~

8

"Here we are, ladies and gentlemen, the venerable Victoria and Albert Museum. Indisputably the finest collection of eclectic oddments to be found under one roof. And incidentally one of fashionable Kensington's finest examples of Victorian architecture in a large public building." With a salute David Heath-Nesbitt gestured toward the grim and turreted facade of the famous institution and indicated that the group follow him inside.

"Please, I'll purchase tickets and pick up floor plans."

"I cannot believe I am standing here," whispered Henrietta Puffenbarger.

"No more than I could believe it yesterday when we walked into Windsor Castle," recalled sister Harriet.

"Dost thou think because thou are virtuous there shall be no more cakes and ale?" teased Arthur Everett. "I'm paraphrasing the Bard, of course. *Twelfth Night*. But why should you not, ladies, enjoy these monuments of mankind, these paragons of pleasure?"

The Puffenbargers twittered nervously and smiled at Arthur. Neither had to remind him that this was their first trip to the British Isles.

"Impressive, isn't it, this entrance hall?" remarked Esther Jenkins, looking all around her. "And one of the ladies we met at Windsor told me not to miss the gift shop here. Said they had the best selection of postcards to be found in London."

Bob Jenkins groaned and feigned a dramatic demise. "But dearest, you've said that in every National Trust place we've visited. Are you going to mail any of those hundred you've purchased?" he asked plaintively.

"You're right about the shop *here*, Esther," chimed Rose. "I always manage a stop whenever I'm in London. And if you need stamps, there is a handy tobacconist on Brompton Road on our way back to the hotel. We pass right by it."

"Thanks, Rose," scoffed Bob Jenkins with mock sarcasm.

"Rose, you are a veritable fountain of knowledge," added Frances Keynes-Livingston. "Do you remember that I'm going to leave you after an hour? I've got an appointment at the laboratory in Chelsea at five. Our week is just flying by; I'm afraid I can't get everything done."

"Thanks for reminding me Frances. Just slip away when you must. I'm sure this is not your first time here any more than it is mine. But as dim and musty as it is, doesn't it feel like you're greeting an old friend when you return?"

"You could be talking about London as well as the V&A. I adore both. And I don't believe one could adequately see every part of London ... or this old shipwreck."

Their guide returned with the tickets and floor plans for each person.

"May I suggest, in the interest of efficient use of our time, that I introduce you to highlights of the museum's outstanding collections? Then, as we did in the British Museum, we shall repair for tea at four. You may roam at will until say, 5:30? Does that suit everyone?"

The company nodded in unison. After nearly four days with David Heath-Nesbitt and trips by boat to Greenwich, Hummer to Windsor Castle, the underground to the British Museum, by foot to Buckingham Palace, the members of Rose's Roamings were ready to march through fire with him. He had sensed their need for pacing and adjusted his pre- planned schedule accordingly. He briefed them thoroughly on each place beforehand and then coaxed their own special interests and expertise to the surface. Always managing to sit with a different person at tea or meals, David took care to spend time with each member of the tour. His understanding and patience and good humor was evident from the outset.

"Now, watch your steps my friends. They keep the lights particularly low here. Say that the bright lights harm the exhibits. Personally, I think they want all visitors to get sleepy and go home so they can close up shop early. Make sure your eyes adjust; it's a perennial twilight."

From room to room they trooped. Coronation gowns, fashions from the 14th century forward, battle armor and weapons, British porcelain through the ages and a dozen other equally formidable rooms: the group received a thorough indoctrination at David's hands. They adjourned eagerly to the cafeteria for a quick tea break at four.

"Sorry, Arthur, no Elgin Marbles today. But I'm sure the Grecian artifacts are of particular interest to you."

"Right they are, David. And Bob Lesley and I are heading that way this minute. See you at the main door at five-thirty."

"Cheers! Now, friends, before you scatter, a bit of a reminder. Do take a look at Tipu's Tiger: it's just down the corridor from here. I'll quiz you about it when we get back to the Currie."

"Do we get extra credit, David?" asked Ellie coyly.

"Indeed! Just want to see how observant this group is. Must keep your wits sharp for the challenges ahead!"

By this time the group had finished their tea and were leaving, each bent on individual missions of inquiry and promising to meet promptly at 5:30.

"Henrietta, I'm going to wander through the costume collection again. Can you believe the innumerable stitches in just one leg 'o mutton sleeve? Or a bustle? Coming, sister?"

"Thank you, dear, but I'm heading for the porcelains. One of those serving dishes was identical to one mother had. I'm going to see if I can get a look at the back of it. I could vouch that it was the Craigamore pattern. You remember, the platter with the sweet little green vine and sprigs of flowers all around it?"

"I do. That was Grosvenor China if I'm not mistaken. But mother's china is far from my thoughts today. I shall see you later, sister, at half-five. Be careful, won't you dear?"

Little did Henrietta think, at this brief parting, that it was *she* who should have admonished her twin to proceed with caution.

~ ~ ~

THE CURRIE STREET HOTEL
Founded 1899

Dear Vinnie and Major:

How we wish you had come with us~! Next Time! Travel is so much easier now, and wheelchairs are the "in" way to go! You'd love our guide: we all do! So interesting and entertaining. All goes well, but we miss you two! Keep W.F. lively until we return!

    Love from the 11 of us!

        xxx Rose

9

Harriet Puffenbarger and Esther Jenkins ambled out of the cafeteria together; leaving Bob Jenkins and Lib Meecham to finish their tea and read the brochures each had collected.

"For someone who has never traveled, Bob is absolutely smitten with this trip," whispered Esther. "Don't you think he's done well, Harriet?"

"Oh, yes," agreed her companion. "No complaints, no falls, no phobias about the sidewalks. And except for Sister, he has outpaced us all."

"Henrietta surely is fit," continued Esther, "and I suppose she credits her golf for that. Sadly, I'm a pansy when it comes to exercise. I don't even join Bob in his daily walks in the Wynfield hallways."

"I'm the same, Esther. But I have to admit I've enjoyed the walking over here. Besides, the weather has been so lovely. Makes me want to be outside. Where do you want to go now? Back to costumes?"

"Shhh, Harriet. If you don't mind, I'm going to the gift shop. I knew if I told Bob he would have a fit. He thinks I've bought too many cards already. Do you want to join me?"

"No, no shopping for me, Esther. You run on. I want to poke around the costumes once more. I'll meet you later."

"Are you sure you know the way, my dear? I hate for you to go off alone…."

"Go on, Esther, before Bob discovers your destination. Of course I can find my way. Shoo! Don't worry about me. I'll see you at the main entrance after five."

And Harriet Puffenbarger began the strangest adventure of her long life. She strolled purposefully down the main corridor in the direction of the costume gallery. But Asian Art beckoned and she wandered for some time among temple columns and the quizzical, silent Buddha whose kindly eyes seemed to follow her every move. From Asia it was an easy progression into Romanesque. She found herself marveling at details on massive carved lintels and statues of the saints. Turning to look for costumes she discovered instead that she was in one of the high-ceilinged rooms with the Raphael cartoons. It was deserted and tomb-like. The guard had long gone for his tea break and, this being the good man's birthday, had lingered in celebration of his day.

Harriet Puffenbarger tiptoed from one charcoal rendering to the next, gazing open-mouthed all the while. *What creative genius could have conceived of such an undertaking? What sort of man was the young Raphael? How did he get that expression on the Madonna's face? What did they stand on in those days to work: simple stepladders like Papa used on the farm?* It was almost too much to comprehend.

"Now let me read this," she said aloud, pausing before a long, faded notice in a glass casing. " 'Cartone is a large piece of paper upon which the artist does his original sketch and may or may not be identical to the completed art work.' And so on and so on about Raphael. Let's see, completed between 1515 and 1516: my, oh my! Lent to the V&A by Her Majesty, the Queen. I *suppose* that this is the present Queen Elizabeth II. And here, the one over here: just as I thought! It's *Christ Charge to Peter*. Matthew 16, verses 18-19. 'Upon this rock I will build my church; and the gates of hell shall not prevail against it. And I will give unto thee the keys of the kingdom of heaven; and....' How very extraordinary that I should remember those verses. Folded away in a wrinkle of my brain from Sunday School some seventy years ago! I must remember to tell Henrietta."

The curious ottoman-*cum*-backrest in the center of the gallery was both unoccupied and inviting. Harriet sat down to ponder the wonders surrounding her.

"Oh, my, this does feel good to take a load off," she said aloud, startling herself with her own echo in the vast and empty hall. She rubbed her left ankle where a wrinkle in her cotton lisle stocking had been bothering her for some time. "I wonder if anyone would object to my taking my shoes off for a moment." She looked around as if to ask permission. Seeing no one, she untied the brown laces of her sturdy walkers and slipped them off. She massaged her insteps. "This does feel good. I'll just sit here a few minutes and then be on my way." She leaned against the padded back of the overgrown ottoman, patted it briskly, and promptly decided it was stuffed with horsehair. *They certainly do not want folks resting indefinitely on this thing. The lights in this gallery are twice as dim as the ones in costumes. Perhaps it's a rule of thumb that the more valuable the contents, the lower the lights.*

Harriet Puffenbarger squinted her eyes and tried to imagine where Raphael might have stood to complete the cartoon on her right. Next she closed her eyes to visualize the many artisans gathering to listen to their master's instructions. And then without effort or expectation the strangest thing happened. Harriet fell into a deep slumber. Her quiet, even breathing barely ruffled the maroon fringe on the cushion behind her head. Five minutes later Harriet was dreaming in Technicolor. She rested her head and stretched out comfortably. When the guard returned he glanced hastily around the silent gallery. The low back of the ottoman obscured the sleeping Harriet Puffenbarger. She had the entire Raphael gallery to herself. She was soon to have the entire Victoria and Albert Museum to herself.

~ ~ ~

When the group gathered at the Cromwell Road entrance at 5:30, Rose and David were both fielding questions and rounding up stragglers who insisted on picking up "just one more card from this marvelous shop". Weary guards smiled indulgently as they held the heavy doors, emphasizing that indeed, it was closing time at the V&A. Rose caught a glimpse of Henrietta's hat as she stood and compared postcards with Esther. Turning, she *thought* she spied Harriet walking out with Bob Lesley. Rose didn't realize that it was Henrietta who had hurried along to catch up with the doctor to ask him his opinion of Tipu's Tiger.

They paused at the Brompton Oratory to listen for a few movements of Vivaldi, then engaged in a fury of postage stamp buying at the tobacconist Rose had mentioned. When Charlie Caldwell and Arthur Everett suggested the group sample the libations at the Bunch o' Grapes across Brompton Road, the idea was greeted with enthusiasm.

"Arthur, this is one of your better ideas," exclaimed Lib Meecham. "We'll appoint you head of the Pub Study Commission for Wynfield Farms."

"Hear, hear," approved Bob Lesley. "You are hereby the official Chair of the PSC."

"David, did I warn you sufficiently about my colleagues? This scandalous group of OAP's." Rose looked at the guide with a twinkle in her eyes.

"Warning? Oh, yes, you warned me, but I think I best start taking it more seriously. To quote old John Gay:

'Fill every glass for wine inspires us,

and fires us with courage, love and joy.'

And the Grapes is an authentic pub; one of the best in this borough. They'll treat us right in there or my name's not worth a cent. This is sampling the heart and pulse of London. Careful now, my friends, cross at the Zebra Crossing. I'll lead the way."

The Bunch 'o Grapes was crowded and the Wynfield residents split up to sit at three different tables, mingling easily with the locals and the other tourists. David took orders and he and Charlie Caldwell moved back and forth from bar to tables and *vice versa* until everyone was sipping their drink of choice and enjoying themselves hugely. The ambience was cheerful and the setting inviting. Voices rose and fell and laughter rippled through the rooms. Strangers became friends and addresses were exchanged. War stories were told and pictures of grandchildren pulled from wallets. The sandy haired bartender kept up a running banter with the Wynfield visitors and bellowed to any newcomer that he was "proud to have so many Americans in the Grapes this very day."

If Miss Moss could see this, reflected Rose, *perhaps it would allay her fears about building a 'public room.' Such camaraderie within these walls*!

"I say, Rose," said David, elbowing his way into a chair next to her own, "I think we're on to something. A good tour of the really old pubs is a must. Why, there's Prospect of Whitby, George Inn, the Cheese...."

"You mean Ye Olde...?" asked Rose.

"Indeed. Though that is too touristy in the spring. Let me work up a list. We'll get Peter to drive us and we can at least see a goodly number in a day or two. What say?"

Rose was thinking that a condensed pub tour, lead by an expert such as David, might be a very fine thing to initiate. Before she could reply, Arthur Everett was solemnly speaking to the crowd.

"Come, my friends, *respice, adspice, prospice.* To the future we must progress. Onward, to the Currie Street, where we shall anoint Rose as Hebe, the Cup Bearer."

Amid groans and giggles and many good-byes the group managed to leave the Grapes and resume their homeward trek.

"You're right, Arthur," Ellie said, "fun as this is, we can't set precedents, can we? Would you look at the time? It is half-past seven already."

When the merrymakers arrived at the hotel they did so in a desultory, tired manner. Clearly everyone was wilting after the burst of spirit at the pub. This had been a full day long before that unscheduled stop. Backs were sagging, knees were beginning to ache, laughs were becoming hollow. Rose could sense rather than see the tiredness. She could also sense that something was not exactly right with Rose's Roamings.

~ ~ ~

10

Once inside the hotel the travelers scattered quickly, picking up their keys from Horace the Concierge and sharing lifts to the upper floors. Alone, Rose stood aside from the desk and frowned thoughtfully.

"I say, Rose, what is it? You do look as if you had just eaten arsenic in your chips. What is it, my dear?"

"Oh, David, I'm sorry I'm such a gloomy Gus. I wish I didn't harbor this queer feeling that something is not right. That some-*one* is missing. Did you count heads when we left the pub?"

"Sorry, Rose, I did not. Caught up in paying the tab and collecting bar towels for Ellie Johnson. Violated my own primary rule: always count heads leaving public places. I did give it a go at the museum. Right as rain there. And I remembered Ms. Frances going on to Chelsea."

"Yes, she had told us about that. Incidentally, while we are on the subject: thank you for treating all of us at the pub. That was beyond the call of duty. From now on, you're *our* guest. I know it was confusing, spread among several tables back there, but I cannot shake this pervading worry. Who could it be?"

"Rose," interjected David, "let us not jump to conclusions. I've never lost a tour member yet. Let me check at the desk and see who picked up keys this evening." He dashed over to the Concierge and returned just as quickly.

"Everyone in, Rose," he beamed. "Even the fair Frances. I say, it is nearly eight in the evening. Would you consider dining with me, Rose McNess?" David Heath-Nesbitt steepled his fingers and looked at Rose with an expression that might well be regarded as imploring.

Rose wavered. The tall, attractive man sent from GENERAL GUIDES loomed in front of her as the manifestation of a dream. This was Someone who could make everything right and good and square again. He could eliminate the tilt in her world and wave anxiety away. Could she really transfer her deepening yoke of foreboding to his shoulders?

"Oh, David, I would enjoy that. But not tonight. I must convince myself that everything is in order here. I am just too unsettled."

"Ah yes, my dear Rose. As the Roman maxim tells us, *abyssus abyssum invocat.* Or, as Mr. Everett would translate, one misstep could lead to something far worse. How may I help? At your service, madam!"

The two guides were beginning to retrace the afternoon's activities when a voice hailed them from the lift.

"Rose! Rose! I'm so glad you're still here. Sister is not back yet!"

"Henrietta! Are you saying that Harriet is *not* up in your room with you?"

"No, no, not in the room, not with Frances, not in the dining room with the others, no where to be found. Oh, I feel terrible about this, just terrible," wailed Henrietta Puffenbarger.

"When did you last see your sister, Miss Puffenbarger?" David's precise voice cut through her wailing.

"I told her at the museum that I ... I thought we should spread ourselves out a bit, spend more time with other members of the group. So we sat with different people at tea and then went our own way afterwards. I wanted to return to porcelains and Harriet ... oh, dear, where did she say she was going?"

"Did she leave the Victoria and Albert with us?" queried Rose. Somehow she knew that Henrietta's answer was going to be a negative.

"I think so...no, wait, did she? I was busy talking with Dr. Lesley. What a lovely man. But sister: could I have missed her? Didn't she come to that pub with us, Rose?"

An exasperated Rose mustered patience and replied: "That, dear Henrietta, is what I am asking you. Oh, I feel as terrible about this as you do. Tell me that Harriet is *not* lost in London."

"Harriet is *not* lost in London, ladies," commanded a smiling David Heath-Nesbitt in his best official take-charge tone. "I'm calling Esther Jenkins: I remember her leaving the cafeteria arm-in-arm with Harriet. She'll know where that good lady was heading. Probably off shopping for surprises for you, Miss Henrietta."

He was back in less than a minute. "Esther Jenkins verified my memory. They did leave together after tea but Harriet wanted to return to costumes and Esther, well, I have no idea where she went. That is the last she remembers having seen her."

"Oh, David, you don't suppose ... no, that could never happen...."

"What, Rose? What are you thinking?" quivered Henrietta, wringing her linen handkerchief into a sodden and useless knot.

"I am thinking that perhaps Harriet Puffenbarger is locked inside the Victoria and Albert Museum. For the night."

"Nigh on impossible," spoke David, "but if the impossible is probable, she is ten times safer there than wandering the streets that are foreign to her at nearly nine in the evening. Rose, I'll hail a taxi and we'll pack off to the V&A as soon as possible."

"Henrietta, you stay right here, in the lobby, and wait for … well, Harriet just might come through those doors any moment and need a stiff sherry when she does. I'll get Cyril to sit here with you." Rose sensed that the presence of elderly, taciturn Cyril might be the calming balm that Henrietta's jangled nerves needed.

Outside, David shouted for the first passing taxi he saw. He and Rose jumped into the rear leather seat of the efficient antiquity and David crisply issued directions to the driver.

They were quick to arrive and just as quick to verify the obvious: the V&A had closed at half-past five.

"What now, guv?" asked the amiable cabbie. "Shall I be waitin' for ye?"

"Righto," chirped David, once again feeling helpless. Action. Action was called for. But how to get this manifestation of British culture reopened at this hour?

"Rose, now listen to me. Do not be discouraged. I've got an idea. Remember what I said earlier?"

"I know, I know: you've never lost a tourist yet. But I still feel terrible. Harriet is such a fragile soul and I *am* responsible for my flock. Have you never lost anyone? Oh, this puts a damper on everything." For the first time in more years than she could count, Rose felt the burning rush of tears welling up behind her eyes. If she started now…

"Now Rose McNess, listen to me," David said firmly. He took both Rose's hands and clasped them between his two large ones, looking directly into her eyes as he did so. "Harriet Puffenbarger is going to be found and she is going to be trim as Dick Whittington's cat. She knew what she was doing in coming on this junket. So far she's been a trooper. She may have become disoriented but my guess is she will be just fine when we find her. And we *shall* find her. Think of all the bragging rights she'll have among her friends: spending half the night in the V&A. Now, my dear, no tears. Tears never help. Let me see if I might rouse a security guard. We'll storm the place and do a thorough search."

British security was never tighter than at the Victoria and Albert on this particular evening. It took an hour of earnest pleading, lengthy explaining, telephoning to superiors, and finally the arrival of a special contingent from Scotland Yard before Rose and David were once more admitted to the museum. It was now eleven o'clock.

The official from Scotland Yard thought it best that Rose and David wait by the entrance desk. "Your friend might hear the commotion and come flying out of the dark like a bat. Reassure her to see a familiar face when she does."

If she does, thought Rose. *I pray that she comes flying out of there.*

"Thank you officer. We'll be happy to stand right here. She told one of our group that she wanted to return to costumes. Maybe try there first?"

"Sorry; Henderson checked there, Ma'am. No sign of 'er. Taking in the lower galleries now, they are."

Another hour of this dark night passed slowly.

As midnight approached an enterprising Scotland Yard man retraced his steps through the entirety of the Raphael galleries. He tapped the sleeping Harriet gently on her shoulder. He tapped twice again before she roused herself from a sleep full of dreams and wonders. Bewildered, reticent Harriet reminded the constable of his eighty-two year old granny in Tollesbury, East Anglia. Without a second of hesitation he helped her to a seated position and then dropped to one knee to coax her shoes back upon her feet.

"And this 'ere's Sleepin' Beauty, folks," exclaimed the proud constable as he escorted Harriet back to the entrance hall and into Rose's arms.

"Harriet, I am so glad to see you! You don't know just *how* glad!" Rose hugged her friend tightly and gave her a kiss on both cheeks.

"And that goes for me, also, Miss Harriet. Worried about you, alone in here with Tipu's Tiger." David winked at Harriet and was rewarded with a sleepy, shy smile.

"But … I just sat down for a moment … and I looked around and no one was looking so I slipped my oxfords off to rest a bit … Why, it's dark outside. I must have slept…."

Rose said her thank you's to all of the guards, the museum officials, the eight constables. Then she accepted Scotland Yard's offer of a ride to the Currie Street Hotel. David climbed in the rear of the waiting taxi and waved his good-bye until the morning. Wisely, he thought it best that Rose alone talk with her lost sheep. He would hear the tale later.

"Rose, you're not going to scold me? I've ruined your afternoon. What could I have been thinking of? I never nap. I had no intention of falling asleep in there. I feel terrible about this whole event. You'll never trust me again."

"Harriet, don't say another word. You gave me a scare. You gave all of us a scare, especially poor Henrietta. She feels worse than you! As David said earlier, you were far safer locked in the V&A than if you had been roaming the London streets. Besides, when have you ever been escorted anywhere by Scotland Yard? You're a celebrity, Harriet!"

Returning to the Currie Street Hotel Rose leaned forward to thank the pair of constables once again.

"I don't know what to say, gentlemen, except a heartfelt thank you from both of us."

"Quite all right, Madam. Put a bit of excitement in me night, eh Robbie?" he beamed to his cohort. "We'll be ringing you up in the mornin' to get more particulars for our report. Chief likes to have all details on paper."

"Fine," replied Rose, suddenly realizing how tired she was and happy to avoid giving 'all details' at this hour. "We'll be here until ten tomorrow morning. We all need to sleep in. Good night, gentlemen, and again, thank you so much."

She linked arms with Harriet Puffenbarger and together they slowly mounted the steps to the lobby. To their amazement not only were Henrietta and Cyril waiting patiently, but each of their Wynfield traveling companions. Arrayed in colorful, exotic styles of night dress that ranged from plain and practical to bizarre and *outre*, they resembled a gaggle of rare birds on a wire. The extravagant aviary was just the tonic Harriet needed to lift her cloud of gloom.

"I am so glad to see every single one of you!" she exclaimed, a wide smile creeping across her face for the first time since she had been rescued.

"Sister," cried Henrietta, "oh, my dear sister. I was so worried. We were all worried. I'll never let you wander off alone again."

Everyone hugged Harriet, who responded by blushing furiously and stammering quietly. There was so much hubbub that anything the good woman might have said would have been lost in the din.

"And Rose," chortled Arthur Everett, resplendent in navy and black striped satin dressing gown with tasseled tie, "Horace asked me to give you this fax. Arrived after you and David left on your mission this evening."

"Oh, you, you … birds! What a welcoming committee! And now a fax. You know what this means, don't you? Kate's faxed me the results of the Wynfield vote. I'll open it in the morning. I can't bear rejection if this is it. Let's all sleep in and I'll give you the results when we gather in the morning. We'll have our breakfast right in our private lounge and won't start out until ten. Everyone needs to get to bed now. Thank you all for waiting up for us!"

More hugs and well-wishes to Harriet and Henrietta, laughter about their various choices of plumage, and finally the last members fled to their rooms.

Rose told Cyril good night and thanked him for his countless games of whist with Henrietta. Ellie Johnson waited patiently until her roommate turned and started for the lifts.

"Rose McNess, if you don't come to bed now I'm going to drag you. I know you must be dead on your feet."

"Bad word choice, Ellie," Rose joked. "You don't know how scared I was that we might find Harriet in that very condition. Let's go up: I can't wait to read Kate's fax."

~ ~ ~

THE CURRIE STREET HOTEL
Founded 1899

London

Dear Annie:

Just a few quick lines but I don't like to bare my soul on a postal card. Hence the letter. Currie Street Hotel is just the same: not one change since you and I were here 4 years ago. Was it really 4 years? I have our old room — they keep room numbers on file forever—and it is as delightful now as it was then. Cyril still creeps around (remember the butler?), Mr. Harley is still the Manager, and Horace is still manning the front desk. We all adore it! Such service and attention. We O.A.P's deserve this! Every one of the group has told me more than once how thankful he or she is to be here. That warms my heart.

Speaking of heart, how is my precious Max? I miss him more than I can tell you. Do call the vet if anything bothers him, but I know that you will. I am surely in your debt for keeping him this long.

Have been incredibly lucky so far with two incidents that could have been disastrous. Both involving Puffenbargers. Rather, Harriet P. First she got locked in the loo at Gatwick, then she fell asleep and spent 6 hours locked in the V&A! I am not making this up: probably made our papers by now; was in the London Times, page 3, right after it happened. Fortunately she has got a sense of humor and was unharmed, nor charged with any crime, so we got off easy on that one! We've had more than a few laughs, let me tell you!

We have a wonderful guide—David Heath-Nesbitt—who is truly gifted. So entertaining AND handsome! We are all smitten with him. He was just marvelous when Harriet was missing, all professional and calm. I needed that! So do not worry about your old mother. I have the ten others, and David, and we look after each other. Especially Harriet P. whom we don't let out of our sight now. Did I tell you this was going to be an adventure? It is that and then some! What do you hear from Tom? Wonder if Kate has heard anything yet. When we left she had not had one peep from him, letter, card or telephone call. A bit rude, if you ask me. My hair is dry now (washed it before sitting down to write this) so I'll sign off. We are off to the theatre tonight and late dinner afterwards. Hug little Max for me and your sweet Jim.

    Love,

      Mother.

(P.S. Don't bother to write: I'll be home before a letter could get to me; besides, we're off to Cambridge and Oxford before long.)

11

"Have you counted them all, Miss Alexander? You didn't forget the stack of absentee ballots that were sealed away in the brown envelope? Are you sure that no one has left a loose ballot on your desk?" Miss Moss was playing the role of Grand Inquisitor and hoping to squelch Kate Alexander's buoyancy.

"They are all here, Miss Moss. With the exception of Miss Hopgood — poor dear — who is too ill to vote, everyone at Wynfield Farms has cast their ballot." She smiled to herself, thinking that perhaps a good stiff drink in the soon-to-be bar would be exactly what Miss Hopgood, and Miss Moss, needed.

"Thank you. I shall now carry them in to the board and have the treasurer count them. And about that letter of yours. Are you *absolutely* certain you wish me to present that to the board?" Miss Moss was vocal in her distaste for the establishment of a "public room" as she persisted in calling it. She was less vocal but more definite in her feelings that Kate Alexander should not leave Wynfield Farms. She had witnessed on numerous occasions the residents' show of affection for Kate, their trust in her word. Kate had a warmth, an outgoing personality that embraced residents and staff alike. She, Elvina Moss, never had nor ever would have that personal touch. She needed Kate in this position of Receptionist. She would be difficult, if not impossible, to replace satisfactorily.

"Absolutely certain, Miss Moss. I composed it this morning. And it is time I moved on. It's the right decision. Please, don't ask me to reconsider."

"Very well, young lady. This will come as a shock to the board, and, I dare say, to members of Mrs. McNess's tour group. When they get back, *if* they get back."

"Oh, they will, never fear. Aren't they wonderful? I've posted all the cards we've received so far. And I've taken calls from the Roanoke and Lexington papers. They want to interview the travelers when they return. Won't they have tales to tell?"

"I shall dictate to you the results of the vote when it is official. This is business information, not a personal message, that we shall be sending. Do you understand what I am saying, Miss Alexander?" With a loud "Humpf!" Miss Moss gathered the large number of ballots and strode into the Wynfield Library for the board meeting.

Kate Alexander pushed back her chair and whistled softly to herself. Since making the decision to move on, she suddenly felt better than she had in weeks. And Albert Warrington's telling her about his nephew in Raleigh had given her a boost. *Tom Brewster can just disappear in San Francisco as far as I'm concerned. He certainly has forgotten me in a hurry, and his grandmother, too. I'll show him I'm not pining away in the hills of Virginia.*

"Now let me see; where is that fax number Mrs. McNess gave me? I promised her I'd fax the results of the vote the minute it was announced. Miss Moss can dictate anything she wants but she cannot dictate the vote. Here it is: Currie Street Hotel. Well, they won't have long to wait now. If Emperor Moss decides she wants folks to know."

What a strange, lonely woman. Certainly I won't encounter many more of her type in my future. Or if I do, I'll be prepared.

Kate allowed herself a few more minutes looking over the tour information Rose had left for her: hotel names in London and Oxford, fax numbers, tour members' next of kin ("Just in case, Kate, but pray I don't have to call you!"), telephone numbers.

"I wonder what those seniors are up to now!" she giggled.

~ ~ ~

12

Rose was humming to herself as she looked around the private lounge that she had requested.

"Thank you, Cyril," she smiled, taking a large tray of assorted pastries from the butler. "This is just perfect. I can't thank you enough. All of our group needed an extra hour's sleep today. After last night...." She shuddered as she shook her head.

"An unfortunate incident, Mrs. McNess. Is the Sister Puffen-barger well this morning?" asked Cyril gravely.

"Probably *very* well, Cyril; all she did was sleep there in the museum. We were the frantic ones. And you were wonderful, by the way, with Henrietta. Did she really beat you at five games of Whist?"

"Indeed," came the reply, somewhat dryly Rose noted.

"For keeping her soothed and entertained, I certainly thank you Cyril. You've done more than enough here this morning. I'll call you when we're all through."

"Yes, Madam," he wheezed affirmatively.

Rose resumed humming and looked over the breakfast selections. *He's got it all: dry cereal for Arthur, porridge for the two Bobs, fresh figs for Charlie and Frances. Milk … let me look: yes, large pitchers of milk and juice. Coffee, teas, hard-boiled eggs. Nothing is lacking. Now I better go over my notes for the day…*

"Rose! Good morning my dear!" Arthur Everett's clipped voice resonated through the sunny lounge and caused Rose to whirl around in surprise.

"Good morning back at you, Arthur. You sound like a man who has enjoyed a good night's sleep. Feeling well, are you? Roommate situation still fine?" *I'll slip this question in just in the off-chance Arthur will reveal something of his relationship with Lib. The way they go their separate ways I'm beginning to think it is all platonic. A pairing of convenience.*

"Top flight, Rose. I'm ready for breakfast and ready for the day. Good idea of yours: we can eat as we plan. Hate to waste too much time going over details again, but then I'm a fine one for telling you that. And especially after last night."

"I'm still feeling guilty about not spending enough time on details with Harriet. Suppose we'd never thought about the woman? What would have happened to her if she'd spent the entire night there alone?"

"Rose McNess, I'm surprised at you even talking like this. Shocked. You didn't sign on to be everyone's keeper on this trip. We are all adults. *Senior* adults. Damn silly thing for her to do if you ask me. Served her right getting locked in there."

"David said the same thing, Arthur, but my conscience nudges me all the same. But I'll show you I'm getting past this. I'll speak of it this morning and that is it. And today, everyone is on his own. I have all the brochures and time tables and bus schedules. Everyone who wants to join us at Hampton Court may do so. The others, well, they've paid their money, they can take their chances. Or choices."

"Atta girl, Rose. That's the spirit I want to hear! Let me tell you that I am not joining the trip to Hampton Court. Been there twice. Must get over to Camden Passage and visit a certain antique map dealer I know. He wrote me about a rare edition of two Cotswold prints from a Buckinghamshire engraver that might be in. Don't want to miss this opportunity. Once in a lifetime sort of thing."

"Arthur, you are a Renaissance man. You have more interests and talents than ten men. No wonder Lib Meecham enjoys your company. There is no book you have not read, no antiquity that you're not an expert on...."

"Lib is a wonderful woman, Rose. Completely self-effacing and far more talented than I. Truly, her company is stimulating."

A bland noncommittal statement if I've ever heard one, thought Rose. *He's closing the door on that subject. O.K. I'll play his game. Just....*

At that moment Cyril burst into the room with as rapid a gait as Rose had ever seen the old butler muster. "Mrs. McNess! The London *Times* is here. They wish to interview you *and* the Sisters Puffenbarger."

"Just send them in, Cyril, there's enough food for everyone. And look, here comes the rest of our merry band."

For fifteen minutes there was an element of confusion approximating bedlam in the now-crowded lounge. The Wynfield group was excited and hungry, and eager for Rose to spill the beans on the contents of Kate's fax. The London TIMES had sent a photographer and a reporter to the Currie Street Hotel as soon as the call came from Scotland Yard. At first Harriet refused their request for a photograph. After consultations with Henrietta, Rose, Esther, and David (who had arrived on the dot of ten for breakfast), she decided that perhaps a photograph might serve as a warning for other older ladies tempted to doze in museums. She sat demurely on a bench in the Currie's elegantly appointed main drawing room, crooked her finger around the handle of a tea cup, and smiled into the camera. Her picture was to appear in the next day's paper on page three.

The reporter who talked at length with Rose and the Puffenbargers was fascinated with the congenial clique of Americans from a pensioners' farm in Virginia. He kept shaking his head in amazement upon hearing the varying ages of the members and listening to the itineraries for their London visit.

"Blimey! Think I've got to join you me'self. Beats what I'm doin' all the day! Mind if I catch up with you in Oxford? This 'er makes a good story. Readers like to 'ear good stories about their country. Makes our tea go down more pleasant."

Rose assured the young man with the unfortunate nose that indeed, he was welcome to 'catch up with them' in Oxford. Her Rose's Roamings was going to be at the Randolph Hotel on Tuesday next. But meanwhile, she had plans to discuss with the group so that this brilliant sunshiny day not be wasted. The journalist and the photographer left with some reluctance.

"Friends, friends, lend me your ear! Now, Arthur, *and* David, no comments, please. We don't need any Latin on top of what we've just endured. First, Harriet, I'm so glad you are no worse for wear this morning. Thank heavens last night's episode is behind us. And that the entire evening had a very happy ending. Harriet, you'll be an instant celebrity when that photo comes out in the *Times* tomorrow! We'll buy dozens of copies and send them to everyone at Wynfield Farms. I'm not going to speak of this near-mishap again. But I do beg each of you to inform your roommate, your companion, *me,* if and when you take off on your own. End of lecture! Now, for the news you have been waiting for...."

"Rose McNess, you have kept us positively on the edge of a precipice all night and morning. Let's hear the verdict!"

"The verdict is YES!" Rose's words were met with a chorus of hearty hurrahs and backslapping cheers from everyone. "It was not unanimous, but a clear majority. Kate was very spare in her wording but did wish us all well. Says life is much the same back at Wynfield. Whatever that can mean! I bet Miss Moss was looking over her shoulder as she typed this fax; that's why it is so brief. Very un-Katish, don't you think?"

"Absolutely. That lovely young creature is too warm to curtail her feelings in a few crisp words. But the important fact is known: Wynfield Farms will have its own pub!" Bob Lesley fairly crowed over his own pronouncement.

"I say, that is stunning news, my friends," joined in David. "Now, who is going to join Peter Bolt and me in the Hummer for an outing to Richmond, Kew Gardens, Hampton Court, and probably a high tea at the Orangery at Kensington Palace? And Miss Harriet, if you would like to take your chances at getting lost once again, we shall point you in the direction of the Maze at Hampton Court. You might stay in the British Isles for another month."

"David! Please don't tease. Seriously, friends, the Hummer will be leaving in fifteen minutes. Time to brush your teeth, grab your cameras, and get back down here. Now who does not plan to go in the Hummer? I think that is easier...."

"You'll be surprised to hear, Rose, that I am off to Hogarth country today," said Lib Meecham. "It is just the sort of clear, cool day that one needs when heading toward his old neighborhood."

"And where is that, Lib?" asked Rose.

"He was born near Smithfield, the city's main meat market. Very poor area. But I've always been fascinated with the humanity and the cruelty in Hogarth's art. Since I'm this close I'm determined to have a look at what formed him. If I get through in time I'll zip on back to Kensington Palace and meet the group for tea. And don't worry, Rose, I have my tube stops all worked out."

"Great!" said Rose.

"Ellie and I are eschewing royalty for the *real* London," confided Frances Keynes-Livingston.

"Just what do you mean by that?" asked Rose, puzzled that her roommate would choose Frances over Peter Bolt and the Hummer.

"We are off for a delicious walking tour of the Bloomsbury area. Don't you think we might be perfect additions to the Bloomsbury Group? I'm hoping that we'll be able to visit the private house and collection of Cecil Woolf."

"And he is?" questioned Rose.

"Leonard Woolf's nephew. Tons of interesting stuff there, and then we'll go on to the Courtauld Institute Galleries. They've moved, you know, but the new location is very convenient. Now don't worry about us, Rose. I think Ellie and I may just be a matched set for this outing!"

"Frances, you and Ellie will have a glorious day. I'm almost ready to give up Hampton Court and come with you. But I've never been to that wonderful old house and I can't pass up this opportunity. And Kew Gardens. So go, go, before I lose my will and make you a three-some."

"Rose, I am off to Camden Passage," Arthur Everett said softly.

"I remember, Arthur. Don't forget to get off at the Angel tube stop. That's a real classic."

"That she is, Rose. I shall see you all back here this evening.

Join me in the Lounge about seven and I'll give you a viewing of my new prints."

"Now Arthur, don't be disappointed if you can't get them to-day," counseled Lib. "I'm sure your dealer will have others later on if these didn't get here."

"I am full of confidence, my dear," shouted Arthur, sprinting down the Currie's steps in the direction of the tube station.

"I say, Rose, after you gather your jumper and Baedeker we shall be off. By my count there shall be eight of us and Peter. A good size and a perfect day. Shall we?"

"I'll be back down here in five minutes, David. The maid is getting ready to Hoover us right out of here if we don't clear. Certainly didn't leave much food for Cyril to return to the kitchen did we? Just like the army: we travel better on full stomachs."

~ ~ ~

13

Arthur Everett strode along Brompton Road at a brisk clip. The spring air was enticing, his mission promising. He breathed deeply and allowed himself a quick appraisal in the glare of a Harrods window. He decided to walk to the Piccadilly tube. Further by several blocks than the Knightsbridge stop closest to the hotel, the walk to the Circus took one past the sweep of Green Park. Arthur enjoyed this landmark and relished the prospect of seeing it again.

Arthur Talcott Everett cut a dashing figure this fine morning. As impeccable in his attire as in his personal life, he wore an ancient but well-cut Harris Tweed jacket in a chevron pattern of light and dark browns. His trousers and polished brogans were a darker brown. A soft yellow tie with blue Scottish thistles brightened his tan shirt and topped the total effect. Because of his extreme baldness and sensitive pate, he always wore a cap or hat when outdoors. Today it was Arthur's favorite: a soft camel's hair cap with a narrow bill. He doffed it often as he passed couples strolling into Green Park.

He tipped it also to the vendors selling various souvenirs and signs along the Park fence. "Good morning to you, gentlemen," he smiled. And it was a good morning.

Crossing Piccadilly Circus he paused for a moment to salute the joyous figure of Eros and then looked toward Shaftsbury Avenue. At this time of day the theatres lining that thoroughfare were closed and quiet, their marquees dark and nearly illegible. He considered briefly purchasing tickets for the new Williamson play. Lib might enjoy that. But was that playing on Shaftsbury or Haymarket? He could not remember. *Ah well, I can look into that after the business at Camden Passage. Best be on my way. Tempus fugit.*

Without a backward glance Arthur descended into the bowels of the Piccadilly tube station. *Piccadilly to King's Cross, change to Northern, Piccadilly to King's, change to Northern.* This became his mantra as he shoved through the turnstile and headed for the train. One was coming into the platform as he rounded the last corner. He followed a large elderly gray-haired woman who was laboriously trying to handle both a small child and a wobbly pushcart of tired vegetables. Arthur helped her load the pushcart onto the car and again doffed his cap. Her grin of gratitude was a satisfying reward. Then he settled into his seat to enjoy the luxury of sitting down for the ride. The exercise had made him feel pleasantly tired but exhilarated. *Perhaps first a spot of tea in Camden Passage. Or even a plate of bangers and mash as the pub fellows call them. Ah, King's Cross already. My stop.*

Arthur left the car, nodding good-bye to the large elderly woman and the toddler as he did so. In his haste to reach the Northern line, Arthur forgot that this was an extremely busy interchange station with trains heading in six or eight directions on two or three separate lines.

He was now part of a jostling crowd hurrying toward an incoming train. He noted the word CAMDEN on a sign above his head and thought to himself, *Home free! Camden Passage and the Angel up ahead.*

Once more Arthur squeezed onto the train behind a number of passengers and managed to find a seat between a very pregnant miniskirted blonde and a tall Nigerian in flowing, colorful robes. Both were dozing, their heads nodding in tempo to the jolts of the moving train. Arthur tried closing his eyes. *Impossible to sleep on one of these trains. Too much noise and too much humanity. Oh my, Camden already.*

Arthur was a happy man leaving the station and entering once more the daylight world above ground. But where was the Angel? Where were the quaint, familiar antique shops so endemic to this region of London? What has happened to the long brick hall of the dealers and the narrow passageways leading off like rabbit warrens? Why was that loud music blaring in his ears? And the purple-haired youths staring at him as he walked along the littered sidewalk … disgusting! Was everyone here dressed in leather? *And that storefront sign that says what: "Navel Piercing"? What has happened here? A canal? There is no canal in Camden Passage. Oh my, I have made a drastic error in calculations. If I could spot a decent youngster to ask directions…. Ugh. Despicable. Earrings, nose rings, tongue rings, half-clothed natives they are. Wait! That seems a likely looking young man polishing his motorcycle. If I dare interrupt his devotion to that machine perhaps he can direct me. I must get out of here.*

"I say, my good friend, I wonder if you could assist me." Arthur hoped that his voice did not betray the sickly-scared feeling he was experiencing in the pit of his stomach. In his whole being if the truth be known.

"*Salve!* 'ow can I help you, me mate?"

"*Salve! Age quod agis!*"

"Don' tell me: you're another Professor Higgins sent to convert me!"

"My dear fellow," a now-smiling Arthur Everett replied, "I am here to convert no one. Literally, I am, as you might perceive, *a fronte praecipitium a tergo lupi.*"

"Blimey! For an old … duck, your Latin's fair good! 'Ow can I help, mate?"

Arthur blinked and started to relax for the first time since setting foot in this place. "For starters, where on this good earth am I? My destination was Camden Passage and some rare and important engravings. Instead, I end up here … God only knows where: I don't! It is something out of Dante's inferno. Can you assist me … ?"

The heavy metal blaring from the speakers above their heads made it necessary for them both to shout.

"Nigel. Nigel Blakely." The tall young man straightened and stuck out his grimy hand to Arthur and they shook vigorously as Arthur Everett gratefully introduced himself. "You, sir, are a *rara avis.* Hardly find anyone speaking the mother tongue now. And not here in Camden Town. 'At's where you are, sir, Camden *Town* and not Camden *Passage.* See those locks over there? Canal runs all the way to the Thames. Used to be major commerce in these parts. Cheap lodgings now. Lots of punks. Say it's comin' back like the Passage. Don' know about that."

"And you, Mr. Blakely…."

"Nigel, please," he grinned. "Me mates never let me live it down if they 'ear you call me *Mister.*"

"Fine. Nigel it shall be. And I am Arthur. But tell me, where did you learn such excellent Latin? You have a real gift with the language."

"Came down from Cambridge last June. Hopin' to 'ear from medical university. You might say this is my *argumentum*. Got to flap m'wings before settlin' down."

"Then we are," Arthur spoke softly, "*Arcades ambo*. I, too, am 'flapping my wings' before settling. You are, my young friend, *virtus probata florescit*: may I call upon your grace to assist me? What is it ... *virtutis fortuna comes*?"

"*Salve*! You mean I'll be good luck to your courage? Right on, Arthur. Name your poison: what may I do to assist you?"

"First, agree to be my guest at lunch at any place of your choosing. Preferably not here. But if you know a decent pub close by.... I've had a vigorous morning."

"*Bonum vinum laetificat cor hominis*. 'Cor! Gentleman like you can't eat around Camden Town. If you don' mind me bike, we'll be off. Happy to accommodate, mate!"

"And after some good wine, Nigel, may I prevail upon you to transport me to Camden Passage?"

"*Viribus unitis*: you and me, guv', we'll be joined at the hip. Hop on, hold tight and off we soar."

Arthur swung his left leg over the rear wheel and clasped Nigel's waist with a firm grip. He kept his eyes focused on Nigel's right earring and tried not to think of the world rushing by. The unlikely pair of Nigel Blakely and Arthur Everett roared out of Camden Town with waves to Nigel's acquaintances and hordes of tourists who stopped to stare at the distinguished gentleman clutching the driver's leather coattails. After a mile, Arthur enjoyed the air rushing past his face and the freewheeling sensation of his first motorcycle ride.

They enjoyed a leisurely lunch in St. John's Wood, an area of London hitherto unexplored by Arthur. Nigel's parents lived in one of the expensive Georgian town houses they passed and the cafe owner greeted Nigel as an old friend.

48 DOUGHTY STREET
DICKENS HOUSE

They dined on *Salad Nicoise, moules mariniers, crêpes avec poulet*, all accompanied by a very dry Vouvret and then capped off with a large serving of apple crumble and cups of strong, black coffee. Arthur once again felt very human and very fortunate. Then he and Nigel embarked for Camden Passage.

"Give me the name of your man, Arthur, and we'll be there in jig time."

Which they were. Arthur inspected Mr. Macallawdie's rare finds and determined that they were the genuine article. Money was exchanged, the maps safely rolled into plastic tubes and Nigel and Arthur remounted and were off to the streets.

"Now, Nigel, you have done more than enough. You may deposit me at the closest tube stop and I shall be out of your hair. I am sure you have many more interesting things to do than ferry this old geezer around."

"Aw, guv, you make me feel like I'm don' a good deed. Take you back to your digs, I will. Can't have you gettin' lost again, not after that lunch. Ever been to Dickens' house? Doughty Street's not far. Let's have a go there and then I'll take you back. Currie Street Hotel. I'll find it. Knightsbridge is not all that toff."

Without a protest Arthur let himself be carried on to 48 Doughty Street and the residence where Dickens spent many of his happiest years with his growing brood.

"Great author, Dickens," mused Arthur Everett, examining the top of the writer's work table. *Labor omnia vincit*: that was surely his motto. And especially poverty."

"At's what m' parents keep preaching at me," Nigel said sadly. Then, brightening up, "But they'll have somethin' to crow about in eight, ten years I reckon."

"What are you planning to specialize in, my young friend?"

"The brain. Neuro. Got to find out what makes 'em tick."

Will wonders never cease, thought Arthur, rubbing his own

head as they made their way down the steep steps and into the street again.

"Currie Street now, guv?" asked Nigel.

"Righto," replied Arthur. "But first, do you know that line from Horace's Odes: *'virginibus puerisque canto'*: I chant to maidens and to boys?"

"Fancied Horace. Sure I do."

"Just let me tell you before we start back that I have thoroughly enjoyed chanting to you Nigel. Not many opportunities, at my age, to chant to maidens. Nor to boys either, for that matter. But your company today has been without peer. *Vita brevis, ars longa.*"

"Life is short, art is long. Not bad, guv. I'll remember that. And don' you worry: my Latin isn't goin' to go. Keeps me sharp."

When Nigel and Arthur roared up to the doors of the Currie Street Hotel, John the Doorman staggered in surprise. His British composure was shaken but not toppled. Coinciding with their arrival was the Hummer's return, Peter Bolt at the wheel and honking wildly for the young man on the motorcycle to move along.

"Stop, Peter! I say, that's a member of our group. Yes, it's Arthur Everett. Indeed!" called David.

Rose had been sitting in the second row and craned her neck for a look. "I don't believe what I am seeing. At least Harriet didn't come crashing home on a motorbike."

To the discomfiture of John, Nigel moved his bike next to the Currie's front doors and stood making his good-bye's with Arthur. The latter seized this opportunity to introduce his new friend to Rose, David, Peter, and the other members of the tour who were slowly exiting the Hummer.

Peter Bolt was running admiring fingers over the Harley and examining its engine in close detail.

"Obviously, Arthur, to look at you I'd say you have had a most successful outing." Rose spoke sincerely, for Arthur Everett, cheeks aflame and eyes shining, had dropped ten years off his age in the pursuit of his beloved engravings. "And you found the prints to be all that you wanted?"

"Rose, my dear, as I have always thought, *vitam regit fortuna non sapientia.*"

"No fair, Arthur," cried Charlie Caldwell, "let us in on your words of wisdom."

"Tell them, Nigel," Arthur directed his young chauffeur.

"Wat the guv's saying makes a lot of sense. Just that 'chance, not wisdom, governs human life.' We 'ad our chances today, dinnit we guv?"

"That we did, Nigel, that we did. And now, *vive vale!* From all of us!"

~ ~ ~

14

It had been a busy day for Rose's Roamings. Despite a late start, they had toured every nook and corner of Hampton Court, from linen-fold panels in the library to the Royal Tennis Court. Happily, no one disappeared in the sprawling maze nor on the enormous lawn surrounding the house. They came away with a healthy respect for the builder, Cardinal Wolsey, Henry the VII who appropriated it, and George II who last used it as royal residence. ("And thank heavens for one of the modern royals who saw to it there are proper toilets in the Ladies!" quipped Esther Jenkins.)

Hampton Court was followed by a visit to charming Richmond, with lunch at an up-scale cafe there, and then a jaunt to Kew Gardens. The group was happy to board the Hummer for the drive to Kensington Palace and tea in the Orangery. Lib Meecham rejoined the travelers and regaled them with tales of her findings in Smithfield. ("Let me just put it succinctly: I am much happier enjoying my Earl Grey tea and sandwiches here with you than I was snooping around in that seamy area of London. No wonder Hogarth had fantasies of death and corruption: it surrounded him in that place three hundred years ago!")

Lib was one of the passengers on the Hummer when Arthur and Nigel Blakely arrived simultaneously at the Currie. She, too, was dumbfounded by Arthur's conveyance and his driver. A few minutes later, standing in the lobby, she, as Rose and the others, was struck with just how vibrant and well Arthur appeared. Obviously she would have much to talk to him about this evening! Thank heavens the young man looked decent, too, in spite of that earring. *Sweet Arthur is so trusting. And gullible. I worried when he told me where he was going this morning; thank heavens he came back unhurt! And looking wonderful!*

By prior arrangement each member of the tour had made separate plans for the evening. Charlie Caldwell, Bob Lesley, and Frances were off to the theatre and a late supper in the Strand. The Puffenbarger sisters opted for a light buffet at the Currie and then an early bedtime ("hair wash night"). Esther and Bob Jenkins had conferred with Rose and David and were venturing to a chic new restaurant in nearby Kensington. Rose had mentioned this particular place because it specialized in Dover sole—'served sixteen different ways'—and Bob Jenkins had been talking about Dover sole since landing in the British Isles. Rose hoped for their sakes that they would just order plain, butter-broiled sole with lemon and not be disappointed. Ellie Johnson had told Rose hurriedly that she was up to her earlobes in Bloomsbury *and* tea and was going to order a drink from the bar and write postcards. Rose knew that Arthur and Lib had much catching up to do. Their looks at each other spoke volumes. They might get to dinner, or again, they might not.

Rose was the only member of her little band who did not have plans for the evening. She was collecting her room key from Horace when David spoke: "Rose, may I have a word?"

"Surely, David. Why don't we sit in the Bar and have a sherry? Do you have time?"

"Actually, I best not. I want to get back and make some calls before we leave on our Oxbridge junket. Day after tomorrow will be here before we know it. But I was thinking …."

"Yes?"

"This is against my personal policy, and rather awkward, but I was wondering…."

Rose wondered also how she could help this suddenly tongue-tied man speak his thoughts.

"I was wondering, rather, that is *hoping*, that you might have a bit of supper with me. Later? After I clear these calls, that is. I did suggest it last evening, you may recall, but then Miss Harriet got lost and…."

"Do not say any more: I remember only too well. It is against *my* policy, too, David, dining alone with my guide. But since I am footloose and fancy free tonight, and we have no one left unaccounted for at either Hampton Court or Richmond, I accept with pleasure! After all, the two of us must keep up our strength." *Does he suspect I am teasing him a teeny bit?*

"Smashing! I was so hoping you'd agree. I'll call and make reservations at London's finest eatery. Just down the block from my flat. I promise you shall not be disappointed. Let me say half-past seven? Will that give you time to freshen up? I could make it later; you say the word, Rose."

"Plenty of time, David. I'll be waiting here in the lobby at 7:30. And hungry. I assure you this London air makes me ravenous."

Rose watched as David Heath-Nesbitt turned and galloped out the door and toward Brompton Road. She had never seen long legs move as rapidly. Rose punched the button marked LIFT and went to her room.

She found Ellie stretched out on the twin bed, snoring. The stack of postcards and pen on the night table were untouched.

Rose shook her friend until she blinked and sat up, rubbing the sleep from her eyes.

"Ellie, wake up. You've got to help me with my attire for the evening. David has asked me out to dinner. Just the two of us! I don't want to get too gussied up but I do want to look, well, decent. Will you have a glass of sherry with me while we talk?"

~ ~ ~

Rose and David had enjoyed a quiet and unhurried dinner and now sipped the strong *demitasse* the waiter had placed before them. There was a quiet complacency at their corner table. Since the evening had begun this was the first lull in the spirited talk they had delighted in sharing. Fellow diners continued conversations and subdued laughter occasionally rang out. It was a restaurant where loud noises were nonexistent and tones were automatically lowered. Rose waited for David to speak but still he sat in companionable silence, smiling tentatively as she took yet another sip of her coffee.

Rose looked around. Even in the dim light she could appreciate the character and charm of the room that both nurtured and protected its patrons. A mixture of Provençal cotton fabric—yellow, blue, red—framed the leaded windows with deep ruffles while racks of antique Quimper ware echoed the riot of colors. Copper ladles and molds gleamed against the pale, roughly plastered walls. Rose thought for the second time this evening that she had been transported to Provence.

"And who is 'The Grenadier's Sister,' David? Has the manager ever revealed her identity?"

"What? Sorry, I was kilometers away. Oh, the 'Sister.' No, sorry, Rose. She's as much a mystery to me as she is to you. But truthfully, did I exaggerate the quality of the cuisine? Was the lamb done to your taste? And the wine: dry enough?"

"The name alone got me, David. I loved it as we walked through the door. It is my kind of place: cozy, quiet, intimate. No wonder you referred to it as your 'special place.' If I had this at my front door I doubt I'd ever fix a sandwich."

"I confess I'm over here quite a bit, Rose. But never with such a delightful companion."

"Thank you, sir. But tell me about yourself, David. You've done nothing but make *me* talk all throughout dinner. Your turn."

"A terribly difficult task, Mrs. McNess: getting you to talk."

"No teasing, David. I'm serious. *Dead* serious as you might say. What about you? Mother? Father? Why the classics? This is not idle chitchat: I really want to know."

"Here goes then, Rose McNess. Mother was the ultimate helpmate: wonderful home manager, enthusiastic gardener, perfect hostess. She met my father when he was stationed in India, and they returned home to London just before the beginning of the war. World War II that is; Father had been a Military Instructor in one of the Indian schools."

"Your father was a military man, I take it?"

"Professionally, yes, but by natural disposition, no. He was educated at Sandhurst, then Oxford. Enjoyed his tenure in India and fully expected to return home and resume teaching. But he was selected to work in Churchill's War Rooms in 1940 and spent the next five years literally underground. Nerve center of the nation, those rooms. Father was an expert on maps. Think what he could do now with computers! At any rate, Mother stayed down in Sussex with my brother and me."

"No wonder you were so insistent that our group tour the Cabinet War Rooms. I can't imagine anyone working in that labyrinth. This is like a story on Masterpiece Theatre. Then what? Did your father retire after the war ended?"

"Heavens, no. We Heath-Nesbitts are long-lived and active. He became Headmaster of a school down in Boxters, Sussex. Public school, of course. Closed the place down when he *did* retire at a healthy seventy-five. Both Mother and Father died within weeks of each other, almost twenty years ago it has been. They were extraordinarily devoted to one another. Lovely parents. I am almost ashamed to admit what a happy childhood I enjoyed."

"Therefore you have no hang-ups." Rose threw this out as a statement and not a question.

"None whatsoever."

"And your course of study: the classics. What prompted that?"

"An obvious choice when your first read-aloud bedtime book was *The Odyssey*. I wanted to read the original Greek and find out about the wanderings of Odysseus. So I grew up and did just that."

"Oh, my, that was a daunting task."

"Not as daunting as trying to gather my courage right now."

"Whatever in the world for? Are you unhappy working with me, David?" Rose was genuinely shocked at his words and furrowed brow. His head was bent over his cup as if he were trying to divine some message in the dark brown liquid. His gray-brown hair fell over his face and he steepled his fingers, balancing tip against tip.

There he goes with those wonderfully long fingers again. Every time he's deep in thought he does that. Where have I gone wrong? Have I pried too much, asked too many questions? But I never touched on the subject of his late wife. I've done something that's for certain. Rose held her breath.

David raised his head, straightened his broad shoulders, and pushed the lank hair back from his face. Once more he smiled at Rose and looked directly into her eyes.

"Rose McNess, will you marry me? There—I've said it!"

"David," Rose spoke slowly, "is this ... this what you've been agonizing over?

"Yes, dear Rose. Will you? Will you marry me? I know I'm no bargain but we both get on so well and seem to enjoy the same things and think so much alike that I just thought it would be brilliant if we were a permanent pair." He paused, breathless, and reached across the pine table and clasped both Rose's hands in his. He continued to smile at her with a shy half-boyish, half-manly smile that caused Rose's stomach to flip-flop despite the large meal she had just eaten.

"David, David," Rose whispered, leaning towards her friend and doing nothing to disturb the pressure of his hands on hers, "you leave me speechless. I'm so ... flattered that I don't know what to say."

"A simple yes would be lovely. And sufficient."

"Oh David, you know nothing is ever simple, not even a 'yes.' I'm so flattered you think so much of me to even speak this way. It's a big step, would be a big step for both of us. I ... I can't say."

"Do you feel the slightest attraction for me, Rose? I hope I've spoken clearly of mine. Well, I am not a man to pour forth romantic sonnets but I hope you know by my asking you to marry me that I find you immensely attractive and ..."

"David, I *do* find you, well, most attractive. You *are*. It's just that...."

"Rose, Rose, stop there. Please. I realize you can't say yes, or no, at this precise moment. Or at least I *hope* you can't say no. But will you at least think about it? We've still got ten glorious days together on our guiding. Promise you'll think about it during these next ten days?"

"Only if you promise not to ask me again during these ten days. I can't afford to let myself be distracted completely, David. I'll promise to think if you promise not to ask. Agreed?"

"Agreed!" he cried, as gleeful as a child just given permission to skip nap time. "Now, let me call for the check and we'll be off. Surely you have time to come up to my flat for a look-round?"

"I don't know, David. Let me get out into that cool, clear air, and get the cobwebs out of my brain. You've got me all unhinged right now. I hate to say good-bye to The Grenadier's Sister. What glorious memories I'll have of this place."

Oh my stars. Pray that Ellie is sound asleep when I get back to the Currie. She can worry secrets out of me faster than a rabbit runs down a hole. I just can't face Ellie with this!

~ ~ ~

THE CURRIE STREET HOTEL
Founded 1899

Dear Paul and Sue—and grands!

Thought about you all today on Fleet Street,

the writers' favorite street in London. Ate

lunch at Sam Johnson's Ye Olde Cheshire

Cheese. Highly overrated & crowded with

tourists (I'm NOT!) but delicious

"ploughman's lunch." Off to Cambridge &

Oxford tomorrow for real dose of culture. Lots

to tell you!

> *Much love to all,*
>
> > *Mother xxxxx*

THE CURRIE STREET HOTEL
Founded 1899

Dear Judy and Rob et als!

Greetings from London! A beautiful time of
year to see everything. Grand group of
travelers with me and we ARE being careful.
Do not worry! Off to new British Library soon
to look up more family trees. So much to do
in 2 (now) short weeks. Give my
grandchildren HUGS & KISSES!

      Love,

        Mother xxxxxxxxx

15

Rose awoke the next morning with renewed energy and a craving for strong black coffee. She had to agree with Ellie: for the moment she was saturated with tea. She avoided her roommate's questions about her "night on the town" and dispatched the morning tour business with brisk efficiency.

This was the group's last day in London before moving on to two full days each in Cambridge and Oxford. The Currie Street Hotel had agreed to hold their original rooms for arrival back in London. For a small fee, of course, but as everyone was so thoroughly happy with their lodgings any fee was a small price to pay for that convenience. David and Peter Bolt were leading a group to the Cabinet War Rooms while Arthur and Lib were heading to the Globe Theatre on Bankside. The entire group had agreed on gathering at the Tate Gallery for a late luncheon in the grand dining room. David had made reservations for a table with a "superb view of the murals"; afterwards they could view the Turners and any other exhibition they wished to see. Rose felt thoroughly satisfied with the way the day's arrangements had fallen into place.

She had matters other than sightseeing on her mind this day, however. With Frances Keynes-Livingston, they emerged from the St. Pancras tube station and walked to the new British Library. Rose found that her "tourist stride" as she laughingly referred to it, easily kept pace with her companion. Both stepped along in a purposeful, no-nonsense manner, Rose in her best tweed skirt and waterproof Mackintosh, Frances in her long canvas duster.

"We should walk together more at Wynfield, Frances," remarked Rose.

"Indeed we should, but then at home you are always encumbered with Max and I with my binoculars, so we would not move at this invigorating pace."

"True," agreed Rose, "but Max is no encumbrance. I have missed him every day. How he would trot along these city streets. But, I hasten to add, you are more than a satisfactory substitute."

They both laughed, then turned into the entrance of the sprawling new library.

"Certainly is impressive," Frances noted. "Apparently the Queen loves it but Prince Charles thinks it is banal and commonplace."

"But then he is vigorously opposed to the 'modernization of London's architecture.' I suspect that this is going to prove to be a very workable library. Well, we'll soon find out," Rose stated.

"Since we are both in pursuit of vastly different subjects, may I suggest, Rose, that we meet here at the entrance in two hours? That will give us ample time to get to the Tate by two this afternoon. Isn't that the time David asked us to be there? Will that give you enough time?"

"Oh I should think so, Frances. Ample. If not, I'll meet you and wave you on. I don't want to spend a whole day here. It's the

Wynfield genealogy I'm tracking down. I took care of my own on my last trip to London."

"Then it's agreed," waved her friend. "My lichens are all in a different section, so I'll say good-bye and be off. See you in two hours. Good luck!"

Rose unbuttoned her heavy Mackintosh and filled out the proper forms at the giant Information Desk. She took a seat nearby and waited for her name to be called.

It was not a long wait. The smiling matron who took Rose's request form busied about behind the desk, vanished a few minutes, and returned with a piece of paper in her hands. She sang out, "McNess" in a chirpy voice and beamed broadly. *What a pleasant surprise*, thought Rose. *She looks as if she is getting ready to offer me sticky buns and hot chocolate in her own cozy parlor, not hand over some dusty research records. She's the grandmotherly type I always hoped to be! Ample bosom, round face, wonderful smile.*

"McNess. Here I am!"

"'Ere you are, deary. One of the lucky ones. Your info all bound together in a folio. Good luck with it, ducks. One of the carrels in the rear is free. Just return in two hours."

Rose smiled her thanks. *She even smells like a grandmother: warm pastry and apple blossoms. I've failed my grands I guess.*

Rose retreated to the first empty carrel she found and placed the leather folio on the small table. After folding her coat and her scarf and putting them on the floor she pulled out the chair and sat down. She extracted the index cards from her purse and uncapped her pen. Sighing, she looked at the folio in front of her.

I am stalling. Get on with it, Rose McNess. Just what in the world am I hoping to find in these pages of history? Family secrets? Mr. Wynfield's bare bones? A hint of Elvina Moss's fam-

ily? No use putting this off: the clock is ticking, literally and figuratively. Let me see ... first Wynfield here in England in 1478: Wynnfosk, from Sweden. Must have come in hopes of finding new fishing grounds and stayed because of the milder climate. Also liked the English women: married 3 times, 11 children, all died in infancy. What sad times those must have been. And hard times. Finally! One son, b. 1488. Jakob Wynnfosk. And he lived a fairly long time: died in 1539. Fathered three sons by two wives. Ummmm. Bad luck with the wives' health it seems. So forth and so forth.... Now! At last we come to the first "Samuel." Must be Grandfather Samuel Jakob Wynfield, b. 1792, d. 1855. Somewhere between the Great-great and the Grand, they changed "fosk" to "field." Must have been assimilating the English language rapidly and that sounded more English. Hmmmm. Samuel J. had two sons, one born 1830, the other, 1831 ... Samuel Thomas Wynfield. That's our Mr. Wynfield!

Rose traced the genealogy with her index finger and scribbled onto her cards as fast as she could. She took a breath and sat back to absorb what she had uncovered.

1831. So Samuel Thomas was a mere stripling of forty-one when he built Wynfield. But when did he come to America ... does it say? Brother Samuel Jakob, Jr. ... the old man liked the name Samuel. Guess he figured if one died, the other would carry on the lineage. And yes ... the brother did die: 1851. Just twenty-one. Probably right out of the University. Let's see, does it tell that? Yes, died of "ague" in University Hospital. What is this? Daughter, also b. 1851. Oh my, I may have just found the missing piece of the Moss' puzzle. This is meatier than I thought. No dry bones here. Let me see: Samuel Thomas sailed to U.S. in 1860, settled in Shenandoah Valley, Virginia. M., 1862, five children, b. 1865, 66, 68, 70, 74. But what happened to his niece? His dead brother's child? And what happened to the brother's wife for heaven's sake. Oh, I'm sure I'm on to something here.

Rose thumbed forward in the yellowing pages until she located the individual family trees of each of the Wynfield sons. Rapidly she read the names long familiar to her from the Wynfield Farms' brochures. *I don't really need to know about Elizabeth, Josephine, Catherine, Mathilde or Samuel T., Jr. ... it's that other putti on the mantel frieze I'm searching for. What happened to her? Bingo! Olivia Ravena Wynfield, b. 1851, Oxford, England; Mother, unknown, died in childbirth, Bermondsey Street Lying-In.*

Mother unknown. Unknown! How do they know the father and not the mother? No one wanted to know the mother, that has to be it. This has to be Miss Moss's great, great grandmother. I can just feel it. Oh, you rascal, Samuel Jakob Wynfield. Probably while you were a student at St. Edmund Hall. You drank, caroused, got some poor town girl in trouble, and never looked back. But who raised this little girl? Who brushed her hair when it was tangled? Who put shoes on her tiny feet and clothes on her shivering body? Did she go to school? Did she get enough to eat?

Rose could feel her heart pounding at this discovery. Her nose dripped and her cheeks flamed. She reached for a Kleenex and sat back again to ponder what she had been reading.

I'm beginning to have a great sympathy for Miss Moss. Elvina. Elvina/Ravena. Could be sort of a name sake I suppose. Well, Baby girl Olivia Ravena stops here. No further information given. I know one thing I'm going to do in Oxford. I'm going to get to the bottom of this mystery if it's the last thing I do. Let me see, are there any Wynfield heirs living near Oxford or in the Cotswolds? Ah ha! One: John William West, grandson of Elizabeth Wynfield. The oldest daughter. Lives in Oxfordshire, in Minster Lovell. Wherever that is. I'm going to call him. Tonight. And I'll ask him to join me for tea when we're there. Perhaps he'll have some clue to the past. Surely the family was told about the other child; they were cousins after all. Part of the family lore;

they were forthright in telling everything else. Probably nothing to them to discover a female offspring in the family tree. A male would be another story: law of primogeniture and all that. Let me get his name down. Would you look, I've almost filled all of my cards.

And then a feeling of total defeat swept over Rose. She felt weak and almost nauseous. Her mouth became dry.

Why is all this so important to me? Just to get to the bottom of the riddle that has been gnawing at me since I moved to Wynfield? To taunt Miss Moss with my knowledge? To confront her with the fact that I, Rose McNess, have found her secret and her hold on Wynfield Farms? To brag to everyone on the tour and blow the whistle on that woman? Oh, no, not this. It's all so sad. A pathetic story. I have a vivid image of that forsaken little girl, Elvina Moss's grandmother or great grandmother. No wonder Miss Moss is so cold and bitter. It has passed down through the years and she can't help being the way she is. No, it is a sick secret and I'll bury it in my heart. The only satisfaction I feel is in having solved the mystery. Now I know who the sixth figure on the mantel frieze has to be! Either out of memory or duty: Mr. Wynfield had her immortalized. My mind is tired; what mind I have left. Would you look at the time? My two hours are practically up. I shall be happy to return these pages to the matron at the desk.

Rose sighed and stretched. Then she stood, gathered her notes and her coat and, tucking the folio protectively under her arm, and left the carrel as empty as she had found it. She filled out the "Return" form and handed the book over with a smile. She turned and met Frances Keynes-Livingston walking to the entrance doors.

"Good timing, Rose. Get anything accomplished?"

"Just about what I expected. Some Swedish ancestry in the

Wynfield line, a few name changes along the way. No dramatic discoveries. And you?"

"Some exciting work has been going on in the Forest of Arden. They have detected a microbe that is eating the lichen and just last year developed a spray that will not harm the trees but it is deadly to the dastardly microbe. Absolutely fascinating reading."

Frances was highly excited over her discovery and chattered rapidly about the many scientific consequences she predicted. She did not expect Rose to reply. Rather, she was content to let her knowledge of the exquisite lichen spill out like ball bearings poured from a tumbler.

Rose McNess's mind was focused on Bermondsey Street and the Wynfield grandson she hoped to meet for tea in Oxford. She found that it was sufficient to smile, frown occasionally, and nod agreeably as if she understood every word that Frances was saying.

~ ~ ~

16

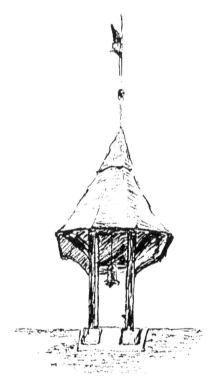

The London sky was gray, dirty dish water with thin soapsuds
clouds scudding across. It was seven in the morning and Peter
Bolt was assisting the Wynfield Farms' travelers into the Hummer.

"Now, m'dear, don'ya look daft today!" he sang cheerfully to
Lib Meecham who hustled out of the Currie Street Hotel balancing a large hatbox and her umbrella. "We're off to Cambridge, 'have you know, not Ascot, m'dear."

Lib ducked her head and smiled winsomely at Peter, never
missing a beat as she stepped into the vehicle.

"About the lot of you, eh Ms. McNess?" he asked Rose.
"Counted eleven, twelve with Mr. David 'ere. Twelve bags under the canvas. Motor on, shall we?"

"That's it, Peter. All down and here by seven in the morning.
Amazing."

"Got our celebrity stowed safely? Gar', dinnit think we'd get out of the Tate yes-tiddy. Must've been a'hunnert folks clamoring to chat up our Ms. Puffenbarger!"

The celebrity status that Harriet Puffenbarger enjoyed as a result of the *Times* photograph completely baffled the shy twin from Botetourt County, Virginia. Everywhere she turned, from the Tate to the Tower of London and Westminster Cathedral, complete strangers approached her. Questions came fast and furiously: 'Not going to forget this trip, are you sister?' and 'Gosh, lady, weren't you scared, locked in that gloomy place?' She took it all with good grace and smiled continuously through the barrage of inquiries. But she had confided to the group at morning tea that she was glad to be leaving London for a few days: "Surely they don't read the London *Times* as avidly in Cambridge and Oxford and I can be invisible again."

"Between you and me, Peter, I think our celebrity is the happiest one in the Hummer today. She is fervently hoping to remain anonymous in the hinterlands of Oxbridge. We'll see how long that lasts: she has secretly enjoyed all this attention." Turning to David Heath-Nesbitt, she whispered, "I must sit by Frances this morning. Promised her I would."

"Understood, Rose. And I have to sit up here by Peter to make sure he takes all the scenic byways to Cambridge. And stops for petrol. Sometimes he forgets to top it off. I'll see you in Ely."

Rose climbed in the rear seat where Frances Keynes-Livingston was holding a seat for her.

"Oh, good, Rose, saving it for you. Move over, Esther, and let Rose get her legs all straightened out."

"I'm fine, you don't have to move an inch Esther. Did you enjoy the Tate yesterday?"

"Glorious, Rose. And the Wallace Collection. And Westminster Abbey ... I could go on and on. This is the trip of my lifetime. Unforgettable."

"I heard that, Esther," piped Bob from the second seat.

"That goes for me, too, Rose. Just an outstanding trip in every way. Awfully glad this is not the road to Gatwick, incidentally."

"Too early for that, Bob. You'll fall in love with Cambridge if I'm not mistaken, and the same thing in Oxford. It will be interesting to me to compare people's reactions to these university cities. Both so similar, and yet so different."

"How about you, Rose? What's your favorite?" Bob Jenkins asked.

"I have to admit," Rose spoke slowly, "that over forty-odd years ago when I was just out of college, an Oxford man met me at Southampton and whisked me up to Oxford in his navy blue Morris Minor. He was studying at Oriel College. I fell in love with the 'dreaming spires and shires of Oxford' and the whole shebang. But not the young man. And I have a special fondness for Cambridge. To me, it's the more rural of the two settings. I like that; it feels, well, cozier. Which it isn't: both Oxford and Cambridge are busy, thriving centers of commerce and business. The universities are just a small part of the industry."

"Rose," Frances spoke earnestly, "you should give the entire group your impressions of Cambridge. And Oxford. You are positively eloquent, my dear, when you speak of them."

"Perhaps I shall," mused Rose. "But now, settle back, we have many miles of chatting ahead of us."

"I've looked forward to this. We really didn't get much opportunity to talk yesterday, did we, to and from the library? I won't press, but I know you uncovered some family skeletons in the Wynfield files. I respect your silence, Rose, and hope that you have gained some measure of satisfaction from your research."

"I have, Frances, and I appreciate your confidence. At a later time, perhaps, I may be able to fill you in on what I've found. Now, new subject."

"My new subject, Rose, is David Heath-Nesbitt. I understand

from Ellie that he has been keeping you quite busy with your un-guide like duties."

"Shhhhhh! Let's keep this conversation very quiet, Frances, and between the two of us. I am going to wring my roommate's neck. I shall. And most likely before we leave Cambridge or Oxford."

"But Ellie indicated...."

"Let me put your mind at rest. David Heath-Nesbitt is a de-lightful man. He has a wonderful sense of adventure and I do find him attractive. Don't we all? But that is it. I did dine with him, alone, the other evening. I'm too old for a fling, Frances. Even if I were offered one. Which has not happened, I assure you."

"Not yet! But I won't speak of it anymore: I respect your feel-ings too much for that. But it is good to sit and talk with you about it. This has been a superb trip. You have done an outstand-ing job of seeing that we've done everything there is to do in London. And I agree: David is an outstanding guide. Best I've run into anywhere, and you know I've been on lots of trips in my lifetime. Why, how he knew about that old professor in the lab in Chelsea is beyond me. I found priceless articles for reference in my book."

"I'm pleased, Frances. You never really take a holiday, do you, from your true love of lichens? But everyone else has. Taken a holiday, I mean, from their phobias, their fears, their buttoned-up selves. This change has definitely worked wonders in each of us. Until today. Maybe we're getting toward the end of our tether, literally. Did you notice how everyone was grumbling as they got in the Hummer?"

"I did hear the twins complaining about their arthritis bother-ing them fiercely. And Bob Lesley was complaining that his hearing aid was on the fritz. Arthur was looking rather dour this morning but I think that is because the concierge didn't have his fresh figs out yet. But it wouldn't be old age if we couldn't complain about it, would it, Rose? And I think the morning's weather has a lot to do with dispositions. This is the first really ugly day we've had on the entire trip. And it's cooler, too."

"Frances, you are absolutely correct. Why didn't I see that? The weather has been glorious up to now. Nothing but blue skies, moderate temps, brief afternoon showers. We've been spoiled. Today is the real English weather. Oh, pray that it improves as we head into Cambridge. I have to confess that my left foot is giving me a fit this morning. Up to now I've had no twinges *anywhere*."

"Shoes fit as they should, Rose? Enough room in the toes?" Frances Keynes-Livingston had worn nothing on the trip except her stout walking boots and considered herself an expert on foot apparel.

"It must be the dampness, not the shoe, that is bothering my foot. But it is bound to get better as the day wears on. That is, if it doesn't actually rain. I've pictured clear and sunny skies in Cambridge, so I can do a bit of sketching. Just hope it turns out that way."

David Heath-Nesbitt interrupted this conversation by calling the group's attention to the surrounding countryside known as the fens, and announced that the bus would be stopping in fifteen minutes for Morning Matins at Ely Cathedral.

"Peter will get us there in ten minutes, in time for a visit to the public loo, and then, if we are quick, Morning Matins with the famed Ely Choir. This is one of the truly great English cathedrals. Since it's so close to Cambridge we surely do not want to miss this opportunity. Doubt if they'll have the thurifer this morning—that's the acolyte who handles the incense—as that is used mostly at Evensong and on Sundays. But you'll still get the rich aroma of the incense: a church that appeals to all of

ELY CATHEDRAL

the senses. Let me tell you one or two things to look for once we're inside...."

"That is why he's such a superb guide, Rose," whispered Frances. "He never misses an opportunity to wangle these little architectural and historical gems in. A walking encyclopedia, that man."

"I agree," nodded Rose, "but he has been doing this a few years. Don't puff the man up too much. He has a considerably good view of himself as it is."

"Methinks the lady protests...."

"All right, Frances, enough. We closed that subject, remember? Oh, here we are, the town of Ely. And there's the cathedral."

The group left the canary-yellow Hummer in a state of eager expectation, their faces wreathed in smiles as bright as the sun that just that moment decided to appear behind the great lantern of Ely Cathedral.

~ ~ ~

17

"Did you enjoy that, Charlie?" asked Rose, settling in her seat as the Hummer left the environs of Ely and headed for the village of Saffron Walden.

"That I did, Rose," came the reply. "I've enjoyed every minute of this escapade. Not that I've been to too many churches. You won't tell on me, will you?"

"Cross my heart. But I'm sure you visited one or two in London."

"Oh yes. I'm fondest, I think, of St. Martin-in-the-Fields, next to Trafalgar…."

"I know where St. Martin-in-the-Fields is located," Rose teased.

"Of course you do. Sorry for the slight. As I said, I'm fondest of St. Martin, then St. Paul's of course, and Chelsea Old Church along Cheyne Walk. Wonderful houses of worship all. But I've enjoyed pleasures of other sorts also, Rose, thanks to David."

"Did you actually go on the pub tour he proposed the other day?"

"Did we! The two Bobs and I teamed up with David and Peter and had a thorough indoctrination of English pub life. I dare say we'll all be fit to serve on the Pub Study Commission when we return home."

The two laughed and watched the countryside roll by. South of Cambridge the landscape was pleasantly hilly. Patches of oil-seed rape dotted the hills with blazes of metallic yellow and the cloyingly sweet smell invaded even the Hummer's closed windows.

"Is that saffron, David?" asked one of the group.

"Oh, no, my dear, rape. Valuable for its oil, and quite brilliant at this time of the year."

"And passin' through right at this time, ladies and gentlemen, one of me favorite small towns in East Anglia: Saffron Walden. In the Middle Ages a hefty pot of gold it was, rich in its cloth trade. Famous for the fall saffron crocus. Find that symbol all over town. Look, there's the old church, one of 'e longest in Essex. Town center over there. Note the half-timbered houses, typical of the day. No time to stop: on to Cambridge fifteen meters ahead."

"And that, my friends, was Saffron Walden according to Peter Bolt," chuckled David. "Right on. We're to check in at The Cambridge Arms at noon. If there are no serious objections I thought we'd go to the Anchor Inn, where the late Sylvia Plath met the late Ted Hughes. Good lunch to be had there among romantic and literary associations. How does that sound? Does it suit you, Rose?"

"Absolutely David. You know of my affection for Plath. I met her once, you know. The Anchor is where Sylvia wore the famous blue head band and…." Rose stopped, realizing that few if any of her friends were vaguely interested.

David winked at her and continued, "And after the Anchor

Peter will pick us up and we'll be off to Grantchester and the 'Old Vicarage' made famous by Rupert Brooke. There's the one line in that poem that every British schoolboy knows by heart. Don't ask me to repeat it verbatim, but it's the line about there always being honey for your tea. And I assure you, my friends, we shall have honey with our tea this afternoon, late. After you have exhausted yourselves on the passages and lanes of charming Cambridge. Ah, here we are: The Cambridge Arms. Once you're settled, say, in thirty minutes tops, we'll gather at the desk and tramp down to the Anchor. Right on the banks of the Granta River. Anyone who wishes may cadge a ride with Peter; he's heading that way also."

"Peter, count on me," volunteered Ellie Johnson. "Save me the front seat."

Hope Ellie is feeling all right, Rose mumbled to herself as she climbed the few steps to the Arms' first floor. *This is an attractive place, more what we'd call a 'boarding house' in the States. Certainly smaller than the Currie but perfectly adequate for one night. We can't get lost, that's for sure. Here it is, our room.* "Ellie! How did you get up here so quickly? Are you all right? Which bed do you want?"

"Happy with either, Rose. Why don't you take the one by the window. I have a sudden headache and I'm going to rest my eyes until it goes away."

"Is there something I can get you, Ellie?"

"No, no, don't fuss. Think cutting down caffeine is doing it to me. I'll have coffee with lunch and that should do it. I took some aspirin; be fine in twenty minutes. I promise."

Ellie was true to her word. She was finer than fine in twenty minutes and became the life of the party at the old Anchor Inn. Afterwards, Peter Bolt drove them to Grantchester where they spent an hour or so walking the sleepy streets, watching the cricket matches in the field, and touring the Church where the clock, according to Brooke, stopped at ten to three.

THATCHED COTTAGES
GRANTCHESTER

When they left the Hummer at Trumpington Street near Pembroke College, David jumped out first and excitedly told the assembled: "We have a treat awaiting us. I've made arrangements with the Vicar to show you something rather special. Follow me."

They trudged through the 14th Century gateway on Trumpington Street and into the building adjacent to the exquisite Chapel. Again, "Follow me."

A Mr. Jonathon Bentham was waiting for them in a paneled room on the first floor. After introductions all around, he explained the great prize awaiting them.

"This, my esteemed visitors, is the first Church that Christopher Wren completed; in deed and in fact, his first building. The Chapel was commissioned for Pembroke by Chris—topher—I should say, Sir Christopher Wren's uncle, Matthew Wren. And we are particularly proud of having in our possession his original charcoal drawings for this Chapel." With that Mr. Bentham opened a seemingly closed panel and revealed

CRICKET WARM-UP
CAMBRIDGE

hanging racks of many large and ancient charcoal drawings from the hand of the great master, the young Sir Christopher Wren.

After oh's and ah's: "And did you say when this Chapel was built, sir?"

"This new Chapel was built between 1663 and 1665. So you may well see the similarities between Pembroke's pride and joy and St. Paul's in London. You are welcome to move closer, to look at the cartoons, but please do not touch. We don't display them openly, but Mr. Heath-Nesbitt said yours was a particularly appreciative group. We are, of course, happy to oblige when we can."

"Sister, here are more *cartoons* for you to examine," Henrietta nudged Harriet.

"Shhh," rebuked Harriet.

"Just another special surprise on our tour, David," said Rose appreciatively. "We all thank you, and Mr. Bentham."

With this delicious *pièce de résistance* tucked away in their memories, the Wynfield eleven sauntered slowly through the

Cambridge afternoon, dodging black-gowned students and bi-cycles. They poked down alleyways, nosed into bookstores and a few even paused to sit along the 'backs' to watch the punting on the Cam.

That night The Cambridge Arms decided that the size of the group warranted a private dining room. It pulled out the best cutlery and china and directed the guests to the square over-flowered, over-papered Best Dining Room. After delicious roast beef and the traditional Yorkshire pudding, followed by a rich steamed sponge cake reeking with sherry, Frances Keynes-Livingston rapped her glass for attention.

"I know we are all stuffed; I am. Stuffed with good food, sights, sounds, historical facts, and not a little bit of fiction. But I think that each of you would be as interested as I was earlier, to hear Rose's impressions of Cambridge. They may have been formed years ago, perhaps, but they ring as true now as they did then. And we have been denied Rose's notes and poetry in our *Wynsong* while we are on this tour. Rose, will you?"

Rose McNess was seated at the opposite end of the table. She stood, pushed back her chair, and began: "Frances is hard to refuse. But I shall be happy to share my impressions only if you indulge my absence tomorrow as I go sketching."

"Hear, hear!"

"Proceed, Rose."

"Thank you. And thank you for your attention. Just a few thoughts, that's all.

"Cambridge is

"... entering through a narrow imposing gate off a busy, noisy street to discover unexpected sweeping vistas of broad lawns, classical buildings and umbrellas of green and leafy shade.

"... walking briskly down lanes and passages, dodging bi-cycles, baby prams, fellows and students fast in serious dis-cussions.

"... sounds of bells from many church towers, especially on Thursdays, when the bell-ringers practice ... sounds of sirens, honking horns, laughter peeling across the Cam, sound of happy pub-goers enjoying their lagers or bitters ... tennis balls being batted over manicured green courts, music floating through open windows.

"... a small town bounded all around by a lazy river no wider than twelve feet across at its broadest ... content to struggle within this self-imposed boundary and living, for the most part, contentedly, hand-in-glove with the University that has been its *raison d'être* since the 11th century.

"... smells of granary bread coming from open windows of a takeaway ... bangers sizzling in the morning ... roast lamb being carved for High Table dinners.

"... a morning symphony of bird calls: the cacophony of twittering sparrows forming the strings, the coo-coo-coo of the doves bringing in the long notes, and the punctuating bassoon of the honking geese.

"... Bleats of sirens through the dark nights, angelic choirs in King's College Chapel ... images of black-gowned masters mincing along College grounds where students must tread only the walkways ... a cream-and-gold coach tied with white satin ribbons, pulled by a matched pair of shiny black horses, driven by a liveried coachmen to a 14th Century church to pick up a bride and groom ... and in the next instant, an elderly man searching through rubbish for a discarded sandwich.

"Cambridge is ... a successful collision of two worlds, the old and the new."

~ ~ ~

Pages from

Rose's

Cambridge

Sketchbook

DOLPHIN ANTIQUES — CAMBRIDGE
33 TRUMPINGTON STREET

PORTUGAL PLACE
CAMBRIDGE

AUNTIE'S
ST. MARY'S PASSAGE

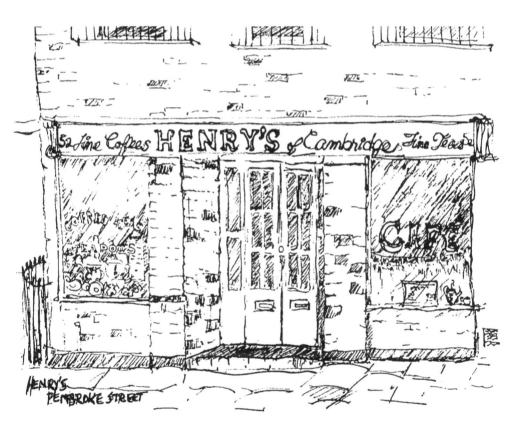

HENRY'S
PEMBROKE STREET

Benet Street
Cambridge

RIVER CAM
from
QUEENS' COLLEGE

LITTLE ST. MARY'S LANE.
CAMBRIDGE

Queens'
Cambridge

SPADE AND BECKET – CAMBRIDGE
"TRADITIONAL BEERS, EXCEPTIONAL FOOD"

WREN LIBRARY
TRINITY COLLEGE – CAMBRIDGE
FROM THE BACKS

THE CAM
from MAGDALENE BRIDGE

BOTOLPH LANE
NO. 16 ~ CAMBRIDGE

KING'S COLLEGE
COURTYARD, LOOKING TO THE BACKS

18

Miss Elvina Moss shook hands with Miss Hopgood's great-nephew and accompanied him to the door of her office.

"Miss Hopgood was a stalwart Christian, Mr. Hopgood. May her soul rest in peace after these past weeks of suffering."

"Actually, Miss Moss, Aunt Lucille enjoyed a pretty full life most of her 97 years. It was only in the last month or so that she failed so quickly. Everything just shut down. The end came faster than we feared. But thank you for your kind words. Did I say that the burial will be in Lynchburg on Thursday? I doubt if anyone from here will be coming. Family certainly doesn't expect it."

"I shall have Miss Alexander post a notice to that effect. And I personally shall inform our residents of the time and place. When Father Caldwell returns from abroad there will undoubtedly be a Memorial Service for her in our Chapel. I am certain he will contact you."

The two nodded amiably and Mr. Hopgood left Wynfield Farms carrying his late aunt's few possessions stuffed into a worn L. L. Bean bag.

Miss Moss walked to the Reception Desk and stopped to stare at the retreating back of Mr. William Hopgood. "Strange how one spends years accumulating things. In the end, everything we own can be portioned out in a bag. Even our bones. But Mr. Hopgood was a very pleasant young man, Miss Alexander. Well educated. And devoted to his great-aunt, or so it would appear. I have no reason to doubt that. Very few of us are fortunate enough to have that devotion in our lives."

Kate Alexander decided against prolonging this subject. *No, I will not try to get inside Miss Moss's psyche. She has shut me out before and it simply is not worth the effort. Must remember that I'm one of the lucky ones. Lucky to be leaving here, too, only not the same way as poor Lucille Hopgood.*

Instead, Kate paused and agreed, "Yes, he did seem pleasant. We spoke a few times this past week. I always hate it when I have to call the families of the sick or deceased, but Mr. Hopgood was here almost the entire time of his aunt's final illness. I'm so glad he was with her at the end. We'll miss her. I told him how much she loved the cook's egg salad sandwiches. That's my most vivid picture of her: loading her plate at tea time and getting one of the girls to carry it to the best seat in the Music Room. Wasn't she one of Wynfield's oldest residents? I mean in terms of residing here?"

"She and Mary Rector arrived at approximately the same time. Yes, you are correct, Miss Alexander. And now they are both gone. Well, you remember the routine. Call Romero and have the apartment fumigated and repainted. Then the utilities checked, carpets cleaned. But I am sure that I do not have to review the check list with you. Now Miss Alexander…."

Kate did not let Miss Moss finish. "Please, Miss Moss, my decision to leave is irrevocable. Same as the pub," she finished brightly.

"Ah yes, the pub," Miss Moss snarled sarcastically. "How could I forget that aberration? Even as we say final good-byes to a resident, construction begins on a new element for the living."

"But isn't that the eternal pattern of life, Miss Moss? We say our good-byes and then our helloes. A ritual of beginnings and endings, birth and death. Change is constant, that's what makes life so ... so *full*, so challenging, so rewarding. Uh oh, I'm beginning to sound like a psych major. And not a very eloquent one at that. Forgive me."

"No need to apologize, Miss Alexander. You have the typical optimistic philosophy of youth. In my opinion *and* experience, and I have had far more years of life than you, change is synonymous with tumult. Introduce new gadgets, new wizardry, and what happens? Instantly everyone becomes an expert and chaos abounds. Look what happened when so many of the residents purchased computers. We were in an uproar for weeks with the telephone company installing new lines, electricians trailing wires up and down the carpets, drilling holes in walls. And the same thing is happening in that, that ... public room. It is a complete mess in there."

Kate stifled a smile. Rose McNess had been the first to own a computer in Wynfield Farms, thereby creating a domino effect. Eleven other residents soon followed her example. The "dirty dozen" as they dubbed themselves emailed back and forth and kept in constant contact with their grandchildren, stock brokers, and major bookstores through this electronic miracle. Kate knew that Rose McNess long had been a thorn and an irritant to Miss Moss. The computer craze and the affirming vote for the pub had just sealed her fate in Miss Moss's eyes.

"I'm sure it will be a charming and much appreciated addition upon completion. Too bad it won't be finished in time for the travelers to christen when they return."

"If they return," sneered Miss Moss. "They are literally flaunting their ages all over the British Isles as far as I can discern. Why, Mrs. Jenkins wrote me a postal card saying that they were leaving for Oxford and Cambridge next week."

"I believe they are there as we speak," replied Kate. "Let's see: yes, the group should be in Cambridge today and tomorrow, and then on to Oxford and the Cotswolds. Golly, I envy them. Don't you, just a bit, Miss Moss?"

"My ancestry is English, Miss Alexander. Oxford, England. From all I have read of my family history it was a bleak and dreary existence and I have no desire whatsoever to learn more of it. Let us speak no more of Oxford."

Kate sensed the distinct chill that enveloped them as Miss Moss spoke these words. "Well, then, I had better call Romero and get busy with my check list. One thing I've liked about this job: never a dull moment."

"Indeed. Do attend to that, Miss Alexander. I shall have letters for you to type this afternoon. We have six people on our waiting list for the Hopgood apartment."

Miss Moss returned to her office. Slumping into her chair she sat a while, resting pointy chin in thin, bony hands. *It would come as no surprise to me to learn that Mrs. McNess took it upon herself to trace the Wynfield lineage when in Oxford. She has hinted at the mysterious sixth child on the mantel frieze since her arrival at Wynfield Farms. What course of action do I pursue now?*

~ ~ ~

19

BIDDEFORD

"Rose! You made it! Peter is bringing the yellow canary around now." Ellie Johnson had no real fear that her roommate might not reappear before departure time but she was relieved when Rose walked into their room in The Cambridge Arms.

"Oh Ellie, I've had the most glorious day. The sweet smell of Spring, blue skies, friendly students. I filled quite a few pages with mostly poor sketches. Let me brush my teeth and grab my bag and I'll meet you at the Hummer. Tell Peter not to leave without me."

"Don't worry, Rose. We'd grind to a halt without you. See you at the car."

When Rose finalized her bill at the desk and joined the others already packed into the Hummer she was greeted by boisterous cries from all.

"And we'll be off to Oxford then, Ms. McNess," shouted Peter Bolt above the refrain. "Should be there before dark. Two hours light ahead of us we have."

"Off to The Randolph Hotel it is, Peter," returned Rose. "They are expecting us after six so we're in good time." Turning in her seat, Rose questioned: "Did everyone fall in love with Cambridge?"

"The *genius loci* of Cambridge, it seems to me, is the ambience of universal learning," declared Arthur Everett.

"I must say that the setting just got to me," sighed Esther Jenkins. "Why, Bob and I walked along the Backs and thought that the scenery couldn't get any lovelier and then it did. From Trinity College to Queens' and that Clare College Garden. Never have I seen such plantings. I imagine in midsummer it is a showcase."

"Oh, Esther, I'm so glad you saw that view of Cambridge. Clare College Garden is a special place in summer. You and Bob did a lot of strolling about then?"

"We surely did, Rose," chimed in Bob Jenkins. "But it might surprise you to hear that we spent a good hour or more in the King's College Chapel. Magnificent place. Heard a splendid organ recital and got in on the end of an excellent guided tour. Why, that building is so spectacular it seems almost to have walls of glass. I'm not one big on architecture as you know, but so far that is the most remarkable building I've seen in England."

"Let's hear it for Bob!" called Charlie Caldwell from the last row in the Hummer. "Good eye, Bob. And Rose, your being a 'Wordsworthian' I'm sure you remember what Wordsworth had to say about it: '… immense/And glorious work of fine intelligence.' A divine intelligence I would say."

"I'm so glad you didn't miss King's. I would have put that on my must-see list if you'd asked me. How about you, Frances? How was your day?"

"Most satisfactory, Rose. Having been here several times previously I more or less wandered at will. Stopped at Emmanuel out of sentimental reasons. I studied there for a summer term many years ago. Not the most fashionable of colleges but a very fine one."

"Frances you sneak! You never told us."

"No need to go into all my past history. Then I sauntered up to Market Hill and the colorful stalls there. So glad progress hasn't pushed everything quaint out of the town. And I stopped at Auntie's Tea Room for a bite of lunch. Rose, there was a wonderful Scottie outside that place. Being walked by a no-nonsense matron who looked firmly in command of her dog. Reminded me of you and Max."

"Please don't mention Max," Rose begged. "How I miss that little devil!"

"Alas," said Bob Lesley, "you won't have much longer before you'll be reunited, Rose. As our friend Arthur persists in reminding us, *tempus fugit*. Five more days of this idyll and then return to reality."

"You're absolutely right, Bob. Two days and nights in Oxford, two back in London and then home again. Anyone homesick?" Rose called to the group.

"Never!" came the spirited reply.

"And now you, Lib," Rose continued, turning to her left. "I've polled everyone except David and the Puffenbargers who love to ride above us *and* you and Arthur. Did you have a good day in Cambridge?"

Lib Meecham blushed before answering. "Oh, yes, Rose, splendid. Arthur and I made a speedy tour of many of the colleges. But our destination was Magdalene College. Spelled with an 'e' on the end to distinguish it from Magdalen at Oxford. The porter stressed that fact so vehemently that it is burned indelibly on my brain. Arthur especially wanted to see the bookcases in the Pepys Library there."

"And did he, Lib?" inquired Charlie Caldwell. "I thought they were open to only a rarefied few."

"Then you may count Arthur as one of those 'rarefied few'," laughed Lib, with Arthur chuckling quietly beside her. "Tell them about it, dear."

"Absolutely smashing. The experience of a lifetime. That library is really something to behold. Includes the famous Pepys' diary in the old boy's own shorthand. Includes an account of Charles II's escape after the battle of Worcester in the King's words, plus a number of other fascinating artifacts. And if that were not enough, a manuscript translation of Ovid's 'Metamorphoses' made for Caxton. If Lib had not insisted on dragging me away, I might be there still, reading to my heart's content."

Rose laughed out loud. "Arthur, to paraphrase poorly the old saying, 'you can take the boy out of the country but you cannot take him out of the Latin.' What a good day!"

"*Res ipsa loquitur*," Arthur solemnly intoned. "Today and tomorrow and tomorrow."

I know what he just said: the facts speak for themselves. Somehow I don't think Arthur is referring solely to today's adventures. He is a sly fox. Rose mulled this over in her mind as the Hummer sped toward Oxford in the fading light. She was content with the independent itineraries her friends had chosen. *Every single person has pursued his or her particular interest or heart's desire. Including me!*

"Did anyone see the Puffenbargers today?" she asked, remembering that they alone had not been checked upon.

"Several times," Lib responded. "After I pulled Arthur away from Magdalene-with-an-e, we strolled aimlessly, down Trumpington Street, over to St. Andrew's and then Regent Street. And we visited several bookstores in some of the narrow passageways. We ran into the Puffenbargers several times. Both of them were carrying wrapped parcels as if they had done serious shopping in Cambridge."

"Maybe that is why the Hummer grows smaller with each

stop," Rose laughed. "Not that we are growing: our acquisitions are."

"It has been a perfect visit, Rose. Just the right amount of time. I had no plans of studying for my Doctorate here." This came from Ellie Johnson, uncharacteristically quiet up to this point.

"Why Ellie, how could I overlook you!" cried her roommate. "Tell us about your day since we are baring our souls here."

"I've had a wonderful day, thank you very much. Went with Bob and Charlie this morning to all the highlights: King's, Trinity, and oh, I forget what all we did see. Then I took myself off to be a lady of leisure."

"That's right, Rose," Bob Lesley spoke up, "she left us on our own for lunch. Couldn't even tempt her with a lager-and-lime."

"Ellie: what did you do? Pamper yourself I hope?" asked Rose.

"Absolutely and completely. I spotted a tiny sign on one of our walks this morning and somehow I was able to find it again. I returned to the 'Fens and Ferns Spa and Bodyworks' and *had* the works: manicure, pedicure, body wrap, facial, hairdo. It was time to take traveler's dust off the old body."

" 'Fens and Ferns' ... what a wonderful name. Oh, I'm delighted for you, Ellie. I know you've been wanting to do this. Sounds like every one of you had a perfect day. I know I did! I'd say we're all indulging our solipsism We'll do this again in Oxford, after David takes us through the hoops tomorrow. I'm glad we've planned on two nights at The Randolph. I am not fond of these one-night stands. Not that The Cambridge Arms was bad. Would you look: Woodstock Road already. Not long now, friends. Oxford, here we are!"

~ ~ ~

The RANDOLPH HOTEL
Oxford, England

Oxford

Dear Jana!

How we would love to have you along with us! Such a lively group and you would add so much! Our guide is an expert on everything from Medieval Sculpture to Italian Opera: you'd love him! We're going to a final concert in Albert Hall when we return to London. Be thinking of you!

Love from Rose and the 'gang'

20

The morning was clear and sunlight streamed into the hotel room shared by Charlie Caldwell and Bob Lesley.

"Bob? Awake over there?" Charlie reached across the gap between the twin beds and punched his friend on the shoulder.

"I am now," grumbled the doctor with good humor. "What *time* is it, anyway?"

"Almost six-thirty. May I fix you some tea?"

"Sure. Drat you, pastor, for keeping me up last evening at bridge. And winning, too. Don't think you gave David one hand, did you?"

"Come now, my friend, it wasn't all my fault. Blame it on the cards."

"All right, all right," he muttered. "Why the Sam Hill are we up so early this morning? We have two full days here. I know there's a lot to see in Oxford but nothing stirs this early. And I don't take that long for my morning toilet."

"Sorry, Bob. I just don't like to waste a minute in this town. Thought we'd take an early morning ramble to the river. I intend to do some punting this afternoon. Was tempted in Cambridge but there wasn't enough time. Always envied those chaps in the engravings, floating along effortlessly with a beautiful maiden languishing in the stern."

"Which do you want to do at this hour: check out the punt or the maiden?" grinned his roommate. "Sorry, Charlie, my legs aren't up to any morning ramble. You go ahead and I'll drink my tea. How about checking to see if The Randolph left us a paper. Hotel this size I'm sure we have a *Times* out there. Or the Oxford *Gazette* or whatever."

"Happy to oblige. And I have a small confession."

"You cheated last night!" exploded Bob gleefully.

"No, no, nothing that scandalous. I'm going to skip David's morning tour. Have an appointment at ten. So I'm going to take a quick peek at some of the colleges now. Plus the river, of course. I'm serious about my punting expedition. If the boatman is there I'll make my reservation now."

Charlie Caldwell finished tying his shoes, gulped the last of his tea, and opened the door to retrieve the newspaper (London *Times*, early edition). He tossed it to Bob Lesley and waved off with a "See you in the dining room around eight!"

As the Reverend Caldwell paused outside The Randolph Hotel to get his bearings, a motorcyclist whipped around the corner and stopped with a roar inches from where he stood. The tall, lean driver hopped off and onto the curb, removed his protective black-and-silver helmet and stood, grinning, before Father Caldwell.

"Morning, Father," he offered, extending his hand as he did so. "It is Father, isn't it?"

"Why, why … yes, yes it is. Father Caldwell. And you are … why yes! You're Arthur's friend from Camden Town. Nigel, is it?"

"Righto, Father. Nigel Blakely. Once of Oxford, once of Camden Town, and now of St. Thomas Teaching Hospital, London."

"You've heard? Why, that's remarkable, Nigel. Arthur will be so proud. You made quite an impression on him last week. Gave the old chap the time of his life. Here in Oxford for any length of time?"

Nigel Blakely dropped his glance and shifted his helmet from one hand to the other. "Well, I have an appointment here at ten so I gave it a go a bit early…."

"Ah," sighed Father Charlie. "I am beginning to understand. Forgive me, it's too early in the morning for me to think logically. You and I, Nigel, shall be co-conspirators at ten, if I am not mistaken. We have the same appointment. But until then, why not enjoy one of the Randolph's 'full English breakfasts' they advertise widely? You must be hungry if you've ridden up from London this morning."

"Planning on that. And could I ask you a favor, Father?"

"Surely, Nigel."

"Could I bother you to use your room afterwards to change into me suit? Leather might give everyun' a fright."

"No bother at all. I'm sure leather wouldn't shock anyone, Nigel, but of course you are welcome to my room. Just ask the Concierge to ring Dr. Lesley in 510. You and he would enjoy a good talk, anyway, I should imagine."

"Thanks, Father. And now for a rasher of…."

"Say, Nigel, before you leave a favor of *you*. Where is the most convenient place for one to reserve a punt for the afternoon? That is one of my ambitions while in Oxford. Can you direct me?"

BRIDGE of SIGHS
- HERTFORD COLLEGE -
OXFORD

CHRIST CHURCH MEADOW
OXFORD

And Father Charlie Caldwell could soon be seen stepping briskly along High Street toward Magdalen Bridge and the boathouses Nigel had indicated. Having secured his reservation, he meant to return to The Randolph leisurely, enjoying the quiet tableaux of St. Edmund Hall, All Soul's, Merton and Oriel Colleges.

The dew was unusually heavy this April morning. The atmosphere was clear and the sky was already as blue as a Dutchman's breeches. All of Oxford glistened with the fire of ten thousand diamonds.

~ ~ ~

Rose and Ellie roused at approximately the same time. They usually did.

"Good morning, roommate," sang Ellie cheerfully. "Glad your friend David is giving us an extra bit of sleep today. He'll probably kill us with a hike all over this town."

"*My* friend David said he was going to show the group every nook and cranny of Oxford. He's a proud alum and he means to show it off. Strap on your hiking boots today, Ellie: you'll need them."

"My Cambridge pedicure was so divine I'll float over the cobblestones. You should try it, Rose. When your feet feel good, you feel good all over. Why not slip away this afternoon and pamper yourself?"

"Thanks, Ellie," Rose replied, gathering up her toiletries and heading for the spacious bathroom. "Actually I have a very important engagement with a handsome older man. Oh, I may as well tell you. The other night I was able to get in touch with Mr. Wynfield's grandson. He lives right outside Oxford and he's agreed to come in and meet me for tea. Perhaps our last day in London we'll be able to schedule a pedicure. My feet will need all the help they can get by that time. Let's book a time at

Harrods and go together. Could you make that appointment, Ellie?"

"Smashing idea, Rose. I will call from here. That is one thing I can do to add to the pleasure of this trip. We'll get the full treatment at Harrods' spa and return to Wynfield Farms looking like tarts! But back to your tea party this afternoon. Why the meeting with Mr. Wynfield's grandson? Or should I ask?"

"You shouldn't but I don't mind telling you. Just polite curiosity I suppose. As long as I was here: why not? And just the normal makeover for me, please Ellie." Rose hoped that she had dismissed the subject of Mr. Wynfield's grandson and stopped to look out the window. It appeared that the day ahead was going to be sunny and crystal clear. There was no sign of rain in that blue sky.

"Well, would you look," an astonished Rose exclaimed. "Ellie, I know my eyes aren't reliable without my contacts but I do believe that is Arthur's friend's motorcycle parked at the curb. I recognize the distinctive handlebars. What was that young man's name? And why would he follow us to Oxford?"

"Might be Mr. Wynfield's grandson. Or have a thing for Arthur," Ellie giggled. "Does have, I should say, if that is really his bike. Lib won't like that one little bit. Nigel: that's it! They were talking about him at dinner last night. Nigel something-or-other. Said he was brilliant and that cockney accent was his way of tweaking his folks. Rather, Arthur was talking about him and Lib was all excited about Colin Dexter."

"The Inspector Morse *Colin Dexter*? Did she meet him?"

"No, but she did invite him to tea. No reply as of yesterday. Concierge told her he comes into the Randolph nearly every day, but hasn't seen him recently."

"Maybe he's out with Inspector Morse," Rose added thoughtfully. "Enterprising of our Lib. I know she reads everything he writes but still, this is quick thinking on her part. But that doesn't explain why Nigel the motorcyclist is here."

"About this rooming arrangement of theirs Rose: did that nearly floor you?"

"How did we segue to this, Ellie? To answer you before I grab the tub first, yes, it did nearly floor me at first. Just think about it. A decade ago it would have been unheard of to travel with some-one other than your spouse or a relative. But at my age I'm not floored for long, and nothing shocks me. And this is hardly a real *shocker*. Lib could not have afforded the trip with that single supplement. They told me that they'd chatted with their respective families and it didn't faze them. So if I wasn't bothered they'd happily share rooms and expenses. Simple practicality. I was so glad they decided to come I didn't give it another thought."

"Good for you, Rose. Frankly I could care less if they shared one room or two, but I suspect something other than practicality. Companionship beats coquetry at our age. Hey, think I should embroider that on a tea towel, dearie: 'Companionship beats coquetry'?"

They both laughed. "Ellie, you are too much. The only thing we have not settled as I stand here shivering is the presence of Mr. Nigel. I just wonder what Lib is going to say when she comes down to breakfast and finds him waiting for Arthur!"

"She'll say 'good morning' … and I say, save me some hot water!"

~ ~ ~

21

The T&J Construction Co., Inc. had set up camp in Wynfield Farms. Four burly men with arms the size of small telephone poles lugged table saws, drills, and various pieces of equipment into the limited confines next to the Dining Room. Since the four men and their excessive girth filled most of the square footage of the room they were expected to transform into a pub, their tools, of necessity, spilled over into the hallway.

This fact escaped neither Miss Moss's notice nor her ire.

"Sirs! Surely it is possible for you to install your equipment in that room. We cannot have this hallway cluttered and filled with sawdust. Many of our residents are highly allergic to dust of any kind and this may be detrimental to their health."

"Lady," said Jimmy the foreman, addressing Miss Moss in a voice weary with explanation, "I'm here to do a job. A job that is hard enough because of the damn low ceiling and the uneven slant of the floor. Tried to get our power saw level in there but hell, worse'n getting a needle through a camel."

Miss Moss allowed herself a small suggestion of a smile.

"I believe that's 'camel through the eye of a needle,' " she offered. "Oh, very well, make all the mess you have to make. I for one will not be around to be responsible for the consequences. But please, could you try to schedule your loudest hammering *between* meals in the Dining Room? That noise would be the greatest distraction to our diners."

"Lady, we've had no complaints any other place we've worked. Me and my crew just want to get the job done, be proud of what we've done, and get out. Soon as we can. And we don't leave no dust behind. We'll try to do the polishing bits while the lunch bell's ringing."

"Thank you, sir. I'll take that on good faith that there shall be *no* dust left behind. And I shall happily leave you to your task."

As Miss Moss returned to her office and closed the door firmly, a second worker approached his boss. "What's with the old dame, Jimmy? Don't like the mess? She ain't seen nothin' yet, has she?"

"Aww, she's probably the head cheese around here. Mr. Ribble up in Richmond warned me about her. Opposed to this whole thing. Said she'd probably try to throw a monkey wrench into anything we'd do. But she's not the one paying the bills so it's back to work. I want to get that paneling up by this evening. Old man Lewis at the mill said the molding was almost finished. We should meet our deadline slick as a whistle. Come on, now."

Major William Featherstone rolled down the hallway, the wheels of his chair making slight crunching sounds as it ran over wood chips and an occasional tacking nail. His eyes sparkled with excitement at the prospect of inspecting this construction project.

"Gentlemen, good morning. I am Major William Featherstone, U.S. Army, retired, and I salute you. Beautiful equipment you have, gentlemen, top of the line. I always judge a craftsman by the tool he carries. You men must be first class. Again, I salute you."

"Thank you, Major," smiled Jimmy, shifting the two-by-four he was carrying and putting out a callused hand to the Major. "Care to come in for a look? Just have to watch the nails."

"Happy to do so, sir. Only reason I rolled down here this morning. Can't wait to see how this small closet is going to become the heart of Wynfield Farms. It will be, you know, the heart of this place. Folks have needed a warmer gathering spot other than the large Dining Room over there. Place to share a bit of the grape and a bite of life."

"Say, you a poet or somethin'? That's pretty good: bit of th' grape and a bite of life. You just think of that?" Jimmy stared appreciatively at the neatly dressed gentleman with the well-barbered mustache who had rolled effortlessly into the cluttered 'closet.'

"No, no," Major Featherstone roared heartily, thoroughly enjoying the compliment. "Just speaking the truth. You know, as one grows older, companionship means everything. And I mean companionship over a cup of tea or glass of stout, and eating one's meager meals and more…. Why, would you believe that I married for the first time this past December? Cuddling has replaced cold feet, snuggling has overcome snoring. Companionship, old chap, that is the key to living. And there'll be plenty of companionship once this pub is completed."

Jimmy Eaton and his three coworkers were silent in their admiration for the visitor.

This old bird must be in his eighties, thought Jimmy. *Retired U.S. Army: he's got to be up there! Damn if I don't agree with him! Love of a good woman means everything.*

"Sure has agreed with you, Sir. Damn if it hadn't. Here, let me show you what we're tryin' to do in here. Think its really going to be nice when we're finished. Me and my boys, we do superior work. Architect's plans got everything spelled out. No way I've been to England. Hardly out of Virginia. But this here is going to be a true English pub or my name's not Jimmy Eaton. See, we've raised the ceiling over here, and the bar is going in along this wall...."

Major Featherstone enjoyed the next fifteen minutes of explanation and exploration. By the time he left all four men had asked him to call them by first name and extracted from him a promise to bring Vinnie down for a similar tour.

As he rolled back along the hallway Jimmy Eaton picked up his square and looked after Major Featherstone. "Damn if that don't beat all. Great old gentleman. Let's get to it boys. We want him to enjoy this as long as he possibly can. He's what makes this place worthwhile, not that complaining old dame up front."

~ ~ ~

The RANDOLPH HOTEL
Oxford, England

Oxford

Dear Miss Moss—

St. Edmund Hall is still standing! Old

Mr. Wynfield would be proud of it. Wish you

could join us here in Oxford! Weather,

sightseeing, guides all wonderful. Here for

two full days. Hope all going well at Wynfield

Farms! See you soon!

    Best regards from

        Rose McN. and the "travelers"

MARTYRS' MONUMENT
OXFORD

Charlie Caldwell explained to the Wynfield travelers that the
wearing of his clerical collar (the first time on the trip) in
Oxford was practically a necessity. There was, after all, the Martyrs' Monument, Bishop Cranmer's memory, and the ecclesiasti-
cal atmosphere that could be *felt* rather than *seen* in so many of
the Colleges. "And also, by the by, I'm meeting some old church
colleagues this morning and I don't want them to think I've
strayed in my retirement." This he had announced to the group
assembled in the lobby of the Randolph as he waved off their
protests for not joining the morning tour.

"Will we see you before tea, Charlie?" inquired Rose. "You
know we'll leave soon after and drive over to The Trout for dinner. David has arranged a special evening in one of his favorite
haunts."

"To be sure, Rose. I'll come back to the hotel after my punting expedition and change before tea. If you want to catch me in the act, be at Magdalen Bridge at three. I should be floating down the Cherwell about that time."

The group roared and followed David and Rose out onto High Street.

"I wouldn't miss that for the world," chuckled Rose. "Ellie, be sure you have film in that fancy camera of yours. Charlie Caldwell punting on the Cherwell is something for the books. Major Featherstone will get a kick out of this. Oh, Lib, did you find out anything about Colin Dexter? Or Detective Morse?"

Lib Meecham looked particularly attractive this morning. The cool English air had put roses in her cheeks and her hair curled softly around her small face. She wore her travel-wise deep blue tweed suit and had added a lustrous blue and coral silk scarf at the neckline. Her lipstick matched the coral touches in the scarf and accentuated her natural coloring. She was, if truth be told, blooming.

"Not even Sergeant Lewis! Everyone at the Randolph tells me that Mr. Dexter comes in every week or so for a meal but never the same day in any week. So they can't say when, or if, he'll appear. I'm so disappointed. You know I wrote and asked him to join us for tea."

"That was enterprising of you, Lib. Your favorite mystery writer and you can't track him down in his own home town. Well, don't give up: he might show yet! And speaking of showing up, where is Arthur? And did I see his young friend from Camden Town in the dining room this morning?"

"Arthur is helping Nigel with some business, Rose. He'll be here in a moment I'm sure. Arthur is such a dear. He promised Nigel he'd look into something and bless me if the fellow didn't ride all the way from London to follow up on it. So Arthur *has* to finish what he started. I'm sure Arthur will join us shortly. Nigel will have to get on back to London this morning."

"Arthur is a dear," agreed Rose. "Well, while you wait for Arthur we'll go on ahead to the Ashmolean Museum. Time waits for no man, nor men, not even Arthur and Nigel. David has a full day planned for us in Oxford. If you get held up for any reason, we're planning to eat at noon at C. S. Lewis' favorite pub, The Angel and the Baby, up in the St. Giles' area. Arthur won't want to miss that—ghosts of all those 'inklings' still lurk there I'm told. See you in a bit, Lib."

Rose waved and followed the others across the street to the entrance of the Ashmolean Museum. After the group disappeared from sight, Arthur and Nigel rushed from The Randolph to join Lib. The trio crossed Magdalen Street and continued their way up Cornmarket to the Town Hall. Charlie Caldwell stood just inside the entrance way.

"Ha! You made it! No one suspects?"

Lib Meecham giggled. "If they do they didn't let on. I've fibbed so much this morning I don't know what is what. Now, we're in your hands, Reverend."

"I told you, my dear, I'll take over here, *de bono et malo*. We go just to the third floor, up these stairs. Awfully decent of you to do this, Charlie. And Nigel. Just swell of you to come all the way from London to stand up for me." Arthur Everett was feeling expansive.

"As you told me back in London, guv, it's *hic et nunc* all's that matter," said Nigel.

"The very least I can do for good friends. We just have to thank a Higher Being for seeing that the papers got here on time. If you'd told me two and a half weeks ago that you were planning to be married, I would have brought the proper chasuble, my wedding prayer book, my...."

"But we had no idea ourselves, Charlie," spoke Lib in her soft voice. "It just happened. We signed on Rose's tour as good friends. Good friends who saw no need to pay for two rooms when we knew we would enjoy each other's company. Isn't that right, Arthur?"

"*Veritas!*"

"And you know Rose told us to bring copies of our birth certificates and all that," Lib continued. "So we each had those. It was just residential status we had to verify. And after the first week in London, we both knew marriage is what we wanted." She giggled again, shyly. "By the time my faxes reach the children we'll be husband and wife. And I couldn't be happier."

"Nor I, my dear. I am the most fortunate of men. Can you believe that she's having me Charlie, Nigel? And on a bad hair day, to boot?"

They burst into gales of laughter. Arthur's shiny pate was the subject of much good humor. When they reached the Clerk's Office they were still laughing and panting after the short climb.

"Indeed," came the crisp tones of the middle-aged clerk who looked up sharply as they entered. "Nerves showing a bit, eh?" She reminded Lib of a third grade teacher she had years ago who took great pleasure in rapping her pupils' knuckles with the worn, petrified tail of a possum. Lib still remembered the sting and the smell.

"Nerves? Not at all, Madam, not at all," Charlie Caldwell reassured her. "*Au contraire*: I would call it more *love* showing. I am Father Caldwell, here to assist today in the union of these two good people."

"Your papers are in order: Mr. Arthur Everett and Mrs. Elizabeth Meecham. Follow me, please. The Magistrate will be in shortly. I see that you have a witness. I shall act as the second witness. Have a seat, here, in this room, and I shall rejoin you shortly. Tea, anyone, while you wait?"

The foursome shook their head.

"These Brits! A cuppa for this, a cuppa for that. The elixir of life, or so they think. A good cuppa cures everything. I hope our Field Marshal there has a cup herself; might put a touch of humor in her," judged Father Charlie.

"*Amor vincit omnia*" intoned Arthur.

"*Amor proximi*," shot back Nigel.

The two scholars clapped each other on the back and enjoyed their collusion. "I hope some day, my young friend, that you are as blessed as I to find such a woman as Lib. *Love does* conquer all."

"Wasn't it Franklin who said it conquered everything 'but poverty and the toothache?'"Father Charlie wondered aloud.

And so, at 10:15 in the morning of a clear and cloudless April day, Lib Meecham and Arthur Everett were united in marriage in the Magistrate's Office in Oxford, England. Charlie Caldwell read the Prayer for a Wedding from the Book of Common Prayer and blessed the ring that Arthur presented to Lib, and then gave the benediction after the Magistrate had pronounced them husband and wife. The no-nonsense clerk hugged Lib warmly and her watery blue eyes were more watery than moist. Nigel Blakely pulled out a large white handkerchief and blew his nose noisily. Charlie Caldwell did likewise, noting as he did that this was the last of his clean handkerchiefs. The corpulent Magistrate *hmmmped* and wheezed and declared that this was a "most pleasurable duty, a fine measure of the day, and could he send out for tea all around?" Once again, the answer was no.

After signing all the necessary registers and papers and getting their passports stamped for the Embassy's satisfaction, Charlie, Nigel, Arthur and Lib walked down to the doorway of the Oxford Town Hall.

"Well, folks, shall we have a celebratory lunch?" offered Charlie.

BLACKWELL'S on BROAD
OXFORD

TOM TOWER
CHRIST CHURCH COLLEGE, OXFORD

SHIP STREET
OXFORD

WALTON STREET
OXFORD

"Got to take me leave, folks," said Nigel, hugging Lib and shaking hands with the groom and the reverend. "St. Thomas is calling me; classes start day after tomorrow. Wouldn't've missed this for the world. Just as you told me, guv, *virtutis fortuna comes.* Now you've got both. *Ave atque vale!*"

"*Vale in pace!*" returned Arthur as Nigel loped away down the street.

"I say again, a celebratory lunch, for the now-three of us?" asked Charlie.

"Love to, old chap, but let me tell you what we have in mind. Lib and I would like this to remain our little secret, until the evening before we embark for home. We're planning a small cocktail party at the Currie before the farewell dinner. We'd like to tell everyone there. If you don't mind, we thought we'd hurry along and catch up with the group. We're bound to run into them at one of the Colleges en route to St. Giles. That way, no one will suspect. I'll say I had to change shoes, or some such excuse. How does that sound?"

"Perfect. I want to do some in-depth studying at the Bodleian Library this morning. Then run over to Blackwell's on Broad to browse. Don't let Lib in there Arthur; you'll never get your bride out!"

"Ha," said Lib smugly, "beat you to it, Charlie! Arthur took me over there last evening and bought me my wedding present. A beautiful leather-bound edition of Rupert Brooke's poems. It was all I could do to keep from telling everyone about it this morning."

"She's more excited about that book than she is me, Charlie. You go right on ahead. If anyone asks, we haven't seen you this morning. Church business and all that. And by golly, you were meeting with church friends, on church business. What could be more important than having you with us as we start our new life together?"

Lib and Arthur strolled off arm in arm in the direction of St. Giles as Charlie Caldwell made his way up Broad Street to the Bodleian Library. Although he was eagerly looking forward to his visit to the imposing library, Charlie Caldwell's main thoughts were focused on his assignation on the river at three this afternoon. *This is going to be a splendid day from start to finish*, he couldn't help telling himself as he busied along the Oxford sidewalks.

~ ~ ~

23

"If only Arthur were here!" cried Bob Lesley, hoisting his half-pint of draft ale and turning to admire the sketches on the walls around him. "After all, we did elect him Chairman of the Pub Study Commission. What better place to start! Where in tarnation do you suppose they are?"

"One good guess would be Blackwell's," said David Heath-Nesbitt. "Arthur has been chatting me up about Blackwell's since we left Cambridge. He'll probably need a steamer trunk to cart his purchases back to Virginia."

"And there is that business with his young friend Nigel. Why in the world would he ride down here all the way from London this morning?" This from Frances Keynes-Livingston.

"Every man—or woman—for himself: that's the motto of my trips," Rose put in. "Lib and Arthur may have decided to tour Oxford on their own."

"Almost makes one suspicious of that Nigel," added Ellie warily.

"Whatever," sighed Rose. "I just know they missed a thorough

indoctrination of the colleges this morning. Especially Jesus College. Did you ever think, in your days of studying Horace and
Ovid, that you'd return here as a guide, David?"

"Never. Only thing I was interested in back in those days was
leaving Oxford. Youth always has to gain more perspective before appreciating one's undergraduate days. Perspective and experience. Once I arrived in Germany I could hardly wait to
return to Oxford. Is that not forever the case?"

"And do I understand correctly that the government has just
initiated tuition for these grand universities?"

"Correct, Bob," replied David. "And 'tis just a fraction of what
I understand your young folks pay in the States. Still, there was
grumbling when they said "no fee, no key" to our ungrateful
louts. Old customs are hard to crack, no matter where … Oh, I
say: here come our wanderers. Lib! Arthur! Over here!"

Lib and Arthur made their way through the lunch crowd in
The Angel and the Baby and toward the back of the pub where
the Wynfield group was seated.

"Arthur, old chap, we were just wishing for you. Missed your
company but we knew you'd want to take note of these singular
surroundings. Transport a bit of the atmosphere to Wynfield if
you can." Bob Lesley beamed at his friend.

"I say, since Lib and Arthur have arrived, may I suggest that we
think about lunch? I'll take our orders up for faster service. We still
have a great deal to cover this afternoon. I want everyone to work
up a real appetite for The Trout this evening," said David.

"I've been trying to remember all we've covered so far," Ellie
remarked idly. She was thumbing through a worn spiral notebook and scribbling as fast as she could. "Jesus, Trinity, New
College. Isn't that a hoot? What was it, founded in 1379? 14th
Century and they still call it new. That was impressive but not
so grand as Hertford and its Bridge of Sighs. I felt as if I were in
Venice once again."

"It's 'Harf'd,' my dear Ellie, '*Harf'd.*' You do want to go back and sound like a proper Oxfordian, don't you?" teased Bob Lesley.

"Thank you, Bob. What would I do without you? Absolutely. I just want to remember where I've been. The old memory's not reliable anymore."

"Ah, friends," called David, rapping the table for attention. "A young maiden to take our orders, if you will." Only the appearance of a snappy barmaid in a short skirt and frilly apron stopped the conversations across the tables and prompted appetites to be heeded.

"Do you think C. S. Lewis and his 'inklings' had as much fun as we are having?" Rose whispered to David over their hefty ploughmans.

"Never!" came his reply. "He didn't have you as his co-worker. Do you really have to tear off to The Randolph this afternoon?"

"I'm sorry, David, but I promised. I told you, I've invited the original Mr. Wynfield's grandson in for tea. Just a gesture of good will, but I think it's important. He may be a doddering old geezer but he accepted my invitation in a snap. While you and the others are tooting around I'll be talking ancient history with Mr. John William West, Esquire."

"And I've planned a brief tea stop at Alice's Tea Shop. Can't come to Oxford without paying homage to C. L. Dodgson. I should imagine that Lewis Carroll is still popular in the States, am I correct?"

"To be sure. Do you know that one of the six original copies of Lewis Carroll's *Alice's Adventures in Wonderland* just sold for $1.54 million in auction in New York City? Can you believe that, for a 19th century piece of literature? Lesser fads come and go, but 'Alice' endures. And speaking of going, we must, David. It is getting on toward two o'clock."

A satisfied and mellow band of tourists from Wynfield Farms

filed happily onto St. Giles Street, Oxford and waited for their guides to direct them hence. Rose stayed with the group until their approach to the massive, classical rotunda that was Radcliffe Camera.

"Ellie, don't forget you're taking pictures of Father Charlie in his punt! He should be returning to the boathouse about four. I hate to miss that sight."

"Thanks for jogging me, Rose. I'll be there, and Esther and Bob want to come, too. We wouldn't miss that for the world."

"Thanks," waved Rose, watching her friends continue up the narrow street with David.

~ ~ ~

Rose trotted briskly to The Randolph Hotel, entering the front doors simultaneously with a tall, distinguished white-haired gentleman making his way slowly with the assistance of an impressive silver-capped cane.

Oh, glory. I have the strangest feeling that this is my guest. Should I say something now? No, I must go to the Ladies to powder my nose and try to look a little less touristy and a lot more genteel, as Miss Moss would put it. Funny, that's the first time I've thought of Miss Moss in days. Wonder if it is prescient?

Rose returned from the Ladies after one swipe of her comb and a blush of lipstick. She approached the gentleman who was sitting in the lobby, both hands resting on his cane, and who appeared to be perfectly content to observe every activity taking place around him at this particular minute.

"Mr. West? It is Mr. West, if I am not mistaken?"

The old gentleman leaned forward, struggling to coordinate the movement of his upper body with his recalcitrant knees. Leaning mightily on his cane he managed to rise to his full height and spoke: "Indeed, John William West, Esquire. And you are Mrs. Rose McNess? A pleasure my dear woman, a pleasure." He bent low and kissed Rose's hand that he still held in his own large one.

What a lovely gentleman. Not that this comes as a surprise.

"And I return the compliment, Mr. West. Shall we? It is tea time all over the British Isles, is it not?"

They walked slowly into the smaller, less formal lounge of The Randolph and Rose ordered their tea. "No, this is my party, Mr. West. Protest all you want but your pounds are of no use here. You are my guest this afternoon."

After the waiter left with the order Mr. West turned in his chair to Rose and asked, "And are you finding your visit to Oxford satisfactory, Mrs. McNess? Weather certainly has been in your favor. Perhaps a bit cool for mid-April, but not the heavy downpours we had last week."

"Everything has been perfect. You must call me 'Rose.' Everyone does. I'll think you are referring to another person when you call me 'Mrs. McNess.' "

"If you will address me as John. I share your feeling: you are talking to my long deceased father."

This exchange broke the ice and they enjoyed a genuine laugh together before tea arrived. The twosome, chatting all the while, did justice to The Randolph Hotel's delicious offerings in the tea department.

After a pleasant lull, with both parties feeling well-sated and comfortably at ease with the world in general, Rose asked: "Tell me, John, about Minster Lovell. Poetic name for a town. Is it far from Oxford? About the same size? And your mother ... oh, I'm sorry, I'm full of questions aren't I? I apologize."

"Nothing to apologize for at all, my dear. I should imagine I have as many questions for you about Wynfield Farms. To be succinct, Minster Lovell is a lovely village. Situated on the Windrush River, oh, I'd venture approximately eighteen meters from Oxford going up the A40 West of Witney. We have the obligatory ancient inn, right on the river, with some ducks that are a damnable nuisance. A 14th Century church. And of course the ruins of the Lovell manor house. My modest cottage is down river just a few meters from all this tourist attraction. You must come and visit, Rose. Would you have time this afternoon?"

"How sweet of you to invite me, John. But I'm afraid I can't. Our real guide, that is, the guide I contracted from GENERAL GUIDES in London, has invited all of us to his farewell dinner at The Trout. I wouldn't have time for a visit before going off with our little group. Do you know The Trout, John?"

"Indeed I do! One of my favorites. For an inn built around 1150 they do a mighty fine job of preserving both antiquity and a fine culinary tradition. You and your friends are in for a rare treat, Rose."

"Why don't you join us, John? The idea just struck me. The others would love it, I know they would. None of us has been there, and I am sure David would welcome you. Our only passing acquaintance with The Trout has been through the Inspector Morse stories. Say you'll come?"

"I'm afraid I must decline, my dear. Sarah, my faithful retainer, is retiring at the end of this month and she is bringing her replacement this evening for me to look over. I fear Sarah would take a dim view if I were to whisk myself off for the evening."

"I'm disappointed but I do understand. One cannot be in two places at once. But I have so much to tell you about Wynfield, and to ask you about your grandfather."

"Why don't you start with the questions? Perhaps then you'd understand more about Old Samuel T."

"Fine," blurted Rose impetuously. "First, what happened to his brother, and the brother's wife? I've read in the family genealogy that Samuel Jakob died at age twenty-one. And his wife died in Bermondsey Street Lying-In Hospital."

"Ah yes, poor woman."

"Does she have a name? Should I go to the Lying-In and look

up her record? Just to complete my study, of course." Rose tried
to convince herself and John West that she had but a passing
interest in the twisted roots of the Wynfield family tree.

"If you should go to the Bermondsey Street Lying-In Hospital
I am afraid all that you would find is a new petrol station.
Chrome and shiny with efficient pumps and officious assistants.
Lying-In Hospital folded decades ago. Plot of earth was sold and
the old building bulldozed. No idea where the records went."

"John, I admit I'm pursuing this for a very selfish reason. I'll
tell you later about that. But did you ever hear your mother
speak of Samuel Jakob's wife? And the child who would have
been your cousin?"

During the pause that followed this question Rose was aware
of a siren blaring in the background. Whether it was her beating
heart reverberating in her brain or an honest-to-goodness siren
she would have been hard put to say. But it continued with its
annoying *whee-onk, whee-onk, whee-onk* for some minutes.

At length, John West spoke. He chose his words delicately.
"Rose, obviously you have done a great deal of research on the
Wynfield family. I sincerely hope out of love and respect for your
place of residence. I, too, am a student of genealogy and in particular, our family's. I am not proud of all parts of it. I can tell,
you, however, that Samuel Jakob Wynfield did the honorable
thing and that my grandfather, Samuel Thomas Wynfield, did an
even more honorable deed."

Rose sat in silence, holding her breath. She waited for John
West to continue.

"Jakob was apparently a genuine rake. Got the local pub
owner's beautiful daughter pregnant. What did they say then: 'in
the family way?' Anyway, got her pregnant. Kate. That was her
name. Kate Slugg."

"What a dreadful last name," Rose sputtered.

"Indeed. And the father's pub was called 'Slugg's End.' English humor, that. To continue, Jakob upped and died after lying drunk on the banks of the Thames all night. That was his honorable act: dying. So it was that my grandfather married Kate to make an honest woman out of her. That was *his* honorable deed. Married not for love, surely, but to prevent besmirching of the family name. Then he quickly got Kate to the Bermondsey Street Lying-In, the clinic for wayward girls, and paid for her to get excellent care. Then *she* died. Leaving Grandfather a widower in name only with a newborn daughter. What choice did he have but find it a foster home? Which he did, and soon thereafter booked passage on a steamer to America. The rest of the story I believe you know."

"I'm overwhelmed," Rose said quietly. "So Samuel T., not the cowardly brother, married the girl to give the child a name. That was an honorable act on the part of a young man. And Kate. At least she had a name. That makes me feel a little better. And ... was the child never heard of again?" she asked hesitantly.

"I recall my late father saying that his father-in-law had made some memorial to the child in the grand manor house in Virginia."

"That would be the carving in the Carrara mantel frieze," said Rose.

"And of course, Samuel sent money to England for many, many years, I understand."

"What about your mother, Elizabeth? She was the eldest of five children so I read."

"My mother died when I was seven years of age. I was raised by my father and a series of nannies."

"I'm sorry," Rose said. "She must have been a lovely woman. There are portraits in the Wynfield Library. Several of all of the children together, and then individual ones. Your mother looked very much like your grandmother as I recall."

"Apparently my grandmother was a great beauty. French. Grandfather met her on the steamer to America. Nice of you to notice the resemblance. But the story does not end here. My father spent hours poring over the family history. The foster family that took in Jakob's daughter came into some sort of small fortune—perhaps from Samuel T's settlement for them—and decided that they would sail for America. Did so, married off the daughter somewhere in the Midwest and *that* is the end of the story as far as I can tell you."

"I think I can fill in the final chapter, John. For your ears only, and certainly nothing I am going to repeat or even put in writing. I am convinced that the daughter—your cousin—had a daughter and then a granddaughter. Does 'Olivia Ravena' ring any sort of bell with you?"

"Ravena! That's it! I knew Kate named her daughter something strange. Ravena: that is the name I heard Father mention in his studies. Heavens knows where *that* came from. Can't think the daughter of a pub owner thought of 'Ravena'. "

"Unless she read a lot of swashbuckling romances, which I doubt they had in those days," laughed Rose. "Well, the daughter or granddaughter or even *great* granddaughter I am thinking of is named Elvina. A. Elvina Moss. And at present she is the Resident Director of Wynfield Farms, *your* grandfather's old home! How's that for irony? Or poetic justice?"

John William West was speechless for the first time since this discourse had begun. "Rose, that is extraordinary. Quite extraordinary indeed." He stroked his generous mustache and stomped his cane on the carpet for emphasis. "Do you think she is aware of this family connection?"

Rose smiled. "I'm sure of it, in her vague, unhappy way. And I'm sure she holds it over certain Board members at Wynfield Farms who are plumb scared to death of what this woman might reveal. She is, if I may speak frankly, a truly miserable, unfulfilled person. She is the proverbial 'round peg in a square hole.' Which is a real tragedy because everyone else in a staff capacity is loving and considerate. Well, most of them."

"You appear to me to be a fixer-upper, Rose. Are you going to share your knowledge with her upon your return to Wynfield Farms in the hope that it might ease her suffering? That perhaps it might make her more content? Maybe knowing that her grandfather's brother was a respectable man would satisfy some longing for acceptance. Many families have far worse black sheep than a drunken father and a fallen mother."

"I may be a fixer-upper, John, but I am going to leave this alone. As you might expect Elvina Moss takes a dim view of me. I'm too cheerful for her, too optimistic. I see the glass half full whereas she sees it empty and bone dry. If she should ever question me, I'd be happy to confide in her. I'd love to say that I'd met you and heard about your home, not that I've given you much of a chance to talk about it. Glory be, would you look at the time?"

"I must ring up my driver, Rose. Too old to drive these busy roads myself. Help me up, would you, my dear? We can chat as we head to the Concierge."

"Gladly, John. Thank you for coming this afternoon. Everything you've told me shall remain locked right here, in secret." Rose patted her heart. "I appreciate your trusting me."

"My dear Rose McNess, of course I trust you. Anyone with enough sense to move into my grandfather's home and make it *her* home has got to have a good mind and the feelings to go with it. Why, if I were about ten years younger I would insist on courting you. Damnable arthritis persists ...."

"Rose! Rose! Whew, thank God you're still here!" Ellie Johnson burst into the Lounge, her face red with exertion.

"Ellie, what in the world has happened?"

"Father Charlie! He fell off the dock and broke his leg. Badly! The ambulance has just taken him to the University Hospital for surgery."

~ ~ ~

24

"A very good morning to you, Miss Moss," called Albert Warrington as he crossed the Wynfield Reception Hall *en route* to his mail box. "Kate not here yet?"

"Miss Alexander had an appointment this morning. You are sounding unusually chipper today. Off on one of your wildlife expeditions I presume?"

"No, no, not today, Miss Moss. Too much work piled up. Several speaking engagements, three large projects to complete in the workroom. I don't allow myself any rambles until I clear my desk, so to speak."

"I did not mean to pry, Mr. Warrington. You know that I am not the sort to meddle into anyone's business. Just thought perhaps your excellent humor was a result of your avocation. Sorry, I did not mean to detain you from your morning's activities."

"You are not detaining me, Miss Moss. Guess I'm feeling chipper because of the progress they're making in the pub. I admire fine workmanship. And those fellows are true craftsmen. Have you noticed the details they're putting into that place? I daresay our English wanderers are not finding workmanship much finer than this in all those musty castles they are visiting. Magnificent tongue-and-groove paneling behind the bar. And a hundred percent old walnut flooring they are recycling. Now that is unique, I tell you. Wynfield Farms will have a conversation piece when this public room is completed. Authentic down to the booths around the wall. If I believed in such things, I'd say Old Man Wynfield is looking down from his perch in Heaven and smiling on this project. What about it, been keeping up with the progress down the hall, Miss Moss?"

"Mr. Warrington, I think my feelings are well known on this subject. This pub as you call it is going to be the downfall of Wynfield Farms."

"Miss Moss, I am a student of Henry David Thoreau. Favorite author. A great man, a simple man. Liked the unadorned life that woods and forests afforded him. One of the quotes I like best from his opus, 'Walden' is: 'Things do not change; we change.' I try constantly to remember that when I encounter the fresh obstacles in my daily life. We must change if we are to keep up on life's treadmill."

"Hmmmph. Thank you, Mr. Warrington, for your treatise on Thoreau this morning. I wonder how he would react to the remodeling taking place. I doubt that he would endorse the drinking and tomfoolery that the public room is going to encourage. Not only encourage but promote!"

"Not familiar with his social habits, Miss Moss, but as I said, he was not afraid of change. Or *to* change if that looked prudent. Good day to you, Miss Moss." With a nod of his head Albert Warrington was once again on his way to the mailboxes.

Things do not change; we change. A lot Mr. Warrington knows about real change, or real obstacles for that matter. They don't know that I've had to change three generations of ingrained habits. They don't know that alcoholism runs in my family as water runs in a river. Does anyone suspect that I am the first to confront and confound that habit? Change? Haven't I done that all my life? Haven't I had to reinvent myself here at Wynfield Farms? But shall I stand by and watch as Wynfield goes through a reversal of fate of which I heartily disapprove? Surely it will lead to excesses of all kinds. Oh, they'll never admit to calling it 'alcoholism' but that is what it shall become. Just one glass of wine, then two, and then ... oh, I know the pattern. Perhaps, perhaps ... it is my turn to make a change. Might my time at Wynfield Farms be coming to an end?

But where would I go? Who wants an aging spinster almost as old as the inmates in a retirement home?

I've always been good with numbers. Mathematics. Yes, I could see myself working with the quiet certainty of numbers. Accounting? A small accounting firm always needs a dependable, older, unmarried assistant.

Oregon? Out near brother? I could call the Chamber of Commerce in Eugene and ask them to forward a listing of accounting firms. Oh, it would be worth all my hard work to see the look on Mrs. McNess's face. If I could only get this arranged before the group returns.... Thought they had Elvina Moss boxed in, did they? Public room for public meeting. Ha! I'll show them a thing or two.

~ ~ ~

25

The cheerful young woman at the Nurse's Station directed Rose down the corridor and to the left. "'Ere's the Waiting Room for surgery. Your chum'll be brought up this floor when Doctor's done. 'Aven't got his room assignment yet. You just 'ave a seat and Doctor will see you presently. Always do."

Rose hurried along the spotless and silent hallway and entered the small, empty cubicle. It was typical of waiting rooms everywhere: flat, dull, cracked, green plaster walls, aging vinyl chairs lined up stoically around the perimeter, tired magazines flung indifferently on a battered square coffee table in one corner.

The difference between this and other waiting rooms Rose had experienced in her lifetime was the profusion of plants. Huge planters of scented geraniums and sweet olive stood in front of the South windows on Rose's right. Sturdy stems reached for the sun nearly two feet up the glass, and the velvety, soft, large green leaves and Matisse-red blossoms tumbled up and out in cheerful masses. The creamy sweet olive mingled happily with the varied hues of geraniums and provided a light relief, almost an orderly punctuation, to the riotous garden.

Rose was immediately drawn to the plants. Inhaling their rich, fruity, slightly-sweet scents she thought of hot summer days and bountiful flower beds.

Someone on this floor really cares about these flowers. Why, they're over 10 years old if they're a day. It must take half a morning just to water and deadhead the blossoms. But how they light up this dreary little room. I'll have a seat. Heaven's knows how long Charlie will be in surgery. Supposed to start at 7. Well, it's half-past now. What is that prayer for travelers Charlie prayed for all of us before we left home? Wish I could recall it now. Little did I think Charlie would the one needing it most! Something like ... 'preserve those who travel and surround them with your loving care ... to the end of the journey.' Well, Charlie, those may not be the exact words but that is what I am praying for you now. Oh, Lord, let him come through this ordeal safely and be returned to us. Amen, amen, amen.

I'm so tired even this unforgiving chair feels comfortable. I must be numb all over: this seat is straight from Stonehenge.

Rose leaned her head back and folded her hands. Closing her eyes she could recount every minute of the past eighteen hours, beginning with Ellie Johnson rushing into The Randolph Hotel with news of Father Charlie's fall.

Rose had bid Mr. West a worried good-bye and grabbed a taxicab with Ellie to the University Hospital. There they were met with the news that Charlie was already sedated and the doctors thought it best to leave him resting. Rose and Ellie had chatted briefly with the surgeon apparently in charge of the case.

All Rose could remember—certainly not the Doctor's name—was "bimalleolar fracture." This, translated the surgeon, meant that Charlie had broken both bones in his right ankle. Badly. And a break that necessitated surgery after the swelling subsided, probably "seven in the morning."

With this glum news Ellie and Rose returned to the travelers waiting at The Randolph. After some discussion it was unani-

BLENHEIM PALACE GROUNDS

mously decided to go on to The Trout as planned. David Heath-Nesbitt had, as Rose explained, "gone to a lot of trouble arranging this dinner for us. Besides, Charlie would insist that we go on ... if he could speak from his hospital bed." At the same meeting Rose decided that the group would tour Blenheim Palace this morning and make a brief foray into the Cotswolds in the afternoon.

"After all, I *am* responsible for each and every one of you and I am not abandoning Charlie. I have been to Blenheim and many villages in the Cotswolds. It's a place you cannot miss. David and Peter and I will decide on a time when you'll return here for your bags, meet me at the hospital and then we'll be off to London as planned. By early afternoon I will have had a talk with Charlie's doctor and I'll know when Charlie will be able to travel."

So Rose had crept noiselessly out of bed at six, thrown what few clothes she had brought into her valise and taken a hotel taxi over to the hospital. She arrived just in time to see the back of Charlie Caldwell's head as his gurney was wheeled into the operating room.

No wonder I am tired. The Trout was marvelous but I can't remember anything I ate but that silky lobster bisque. And cham-

pagne. *That was sweet of David to order flutes of bubbly for all of us. It did raise spirits I admit. His toast was so lovely; I must try to remember that to quote to Charlie. Something by Edmund Spenser ... 'a noble heart that harbours virtuous thought.' How like Charlie that is. Well, I can't stay this glum. Maybe a bite of breakfast would help. Surely I can find a cup of black coffee in that canteen on the first floor. Yes, coffee and something sweet to raise my energy level. And my state of mind. I must put on a cheerful face for everyone's sake. Charlie would forbid this gloom-and-doom.*

Rose stirred herself and went down to the canteen where she did find the sustenance she craved: steaming black coffee in a large china mug and a gooey bun the size of a small loaf of bread. She sat and ate slowly, watching the nurses and visitors who drifted in and out in two's and three's.

What brings these people here at this hour? New babies on the way? Family member clinging to life? A terminally ill parent? There is a story behind every face. But I better be getting back upstairs to my place and my story.

Nine o'clock came and went. Rose dozed. The combination of the flowery perfume and the morning sunshine seduced her into thinking that her present choice of chair, after trying each one of them, was as soft as eiderdown.

At nine-thirty Rose was dreaming of Cornwall and high cliffs and brambles of roses when she heard someone call her name.

"Mrs. McNess? Doctor Powell. I'm sorry to disturb you...."

"Oh, no, I mean, Doctor Powell. Good morning! I am so glad to see you. How is Charlie? I mean, Father Caldwell: how is he?"

"Doing well, doing well. Came through surgery first-rate. Sun and the scent got to you in here, has it?"

"Well," replied Rose, rubbing her eyes, "I have to admit they are a fairly toxic anesthesia. Almost makes one forget these hard chairs and the reason for being here in the first place. But tell me, did the surgery go as you had hoped?"

"Absolutely. Father Caldwell has the constitution and physique of a fifty-year old. Never had a finer patient. Tibia a bit more damaged than the fibula, but we expected that. Two screws, two pints of blood. He's in Recovery now, semi-alert. Talking about Caesar. Is your Father Charlie a student of Latin?"

Rose laughed, her first of the morning. "That's a good sign. No, Caesar is Charlie's African gray parrot back home. I guess that means his memory is in good shape. He must be thinking of getting back to Virginia. I'm almost afraid to ask, Doctor Powell, when do you think Charlie will be able to travel?"

"He's in plaster, of course. Right leg, up to his thigh. Bimalleolar fracture is serious but not life threatening. He'll have to have a wheelchair for the next two, three weeks. I don't recommend crutches or a walker until he is on familiar ground and sees his own doctor in the states. Did I understand that you are the leader of this tour? When are you planning to leave England, Mrs. McNess?"

"You understood correctly, Doctor. I am a sort-of leader in that I instigated this whole affair. And I do feel responsible for every one of my friends. We are Seniors and can certainly manage but...."

"Don't assume the blame for this accident, Mrs. McNess, if that is what you are about to do. Father Charlie could have stepped off a curb and done the same thing to his ankle. Or stepped off and been broadsided by one of our crazy drivers. Just think of the colorful tale the good Father can embroider: punting on the Cherwell, swerving to avoid a maiden, and so forth. For the little I've talked with my patient I can wager that it will be a jolly good story when he gets home."

"You are perceptive, Dr. Powell. How well you read Father Charlie! He is much loved by everyone, especially all of us O.A.P.'s. You really think he'll be up to flying on Friday of this

EN ROUTE — COTSWOLDS

week? I could have wheelchairs arranged for Gatwick and at the other end."

"Friday. Ummm. This is Tuesday. I see no reason why he won't be able to fly with you. Gatwick is not that far. He could get a taxi to deliver him to the proper gate. With instructions, of course, and pain medication if necessary. I'll be following his case closely the rest of today and tomorrow. Barring complications I see no reason not to discharge him on Friday."

"Dr. Powell, you have just made me a happy woman. And I know Father Charlie will be thrilled to hear that news. When can I see him? I'm waiting solely for the purpose of being with him up until four this afternoon."

"What have you done with your fellow travelers, Mrs. McNess?"

"I've sent them on to Blenheim and a bit of the Cotswolds. My real guide and the driver have them in tow. We unanimously decided that Charlie would want us to 'carry on' as you Brits say. I've visited your country many times in the past, so I elected to remain with Charlie. My fellow guide will come up to get me when they return and we'll motor back to London this evening."

"Then I shall leave you, Mrs. McNess. I'll have one of the nurses at the station come and get you when Father Charlie is settled in his room. Shouldn't be much longer. Are you sure you're all right here? Sorry about these chairs. Even the scent of the *Pelargonium gravelens*, alas, doesn't make them any less un-yielding."

"Why, Doctor Powell, are you the horticulturist on this floor?"

"I confess that I am. You are looking at my success cases, Mrs. McNess. I figured that if I could repair broken legs and graft bones, I could do the same things with cuttings. Each one of these plants began life as a slip in a petri dish. Some are as old as my eldest son, and he's a strapping twelve."

"You are to be congratulated, Doctor. Their beauty makes waiting almost a pleasure. If you close your eyes and breathe deeply, you can imagine you are transported to Heaven."

This time it was the doctor's turn to laugh. "Thank you, Mrs. McNess. And speaking of transporting, I must transport myself back to my patient and another surgery or two. It has been a pleasure, Mrs. McNess. I do hope that you won't let this experi-ence ruin your stay in Oxford."

"You have eliminated that probability, Doctor Powell. I can-not thank you enough for looking after my friend so well. If I don't see you again, know that you are more than welcome any time you come to Virginia. And Wynfield Farms."

After Dr. Powell waved and left, Rose sat down once more. Her tiredness had vanished, disappeared as surely as the white-coated doctor had disappeared.

Ah, me, she sighed. *One more time, Lord, one more time we've been lucky. This could have been a tragedy for each and every one of us. To a man they would have thought 'it might have been me' and then be afraid to move. A bad accident but it could not have hap-pened to a nicer man. Thank you Lord, thank you, for bringing Fa-ther Charlie safely to the end of this journey. And while I've got your ear, Lord, please, will you stay with us until we land in Roanoke?*

~ ~ ~

The RANDOLPH HOTEL
Oxford, England

Cambridge, England

Dearest Vinnie,

Just time for a quick note while Ellie is out with Bob Lesley. Those two have had quite a time on this trip! Nothing romantic, mind you, but just enjoyed each other's company. I could never have asked for a more congenial roommate. Ellie wakes up laughing and goes through each day in the same exact manner: happy, agreeable, and plain good fun! But how I wish you were here: I have a real dilemma! We have, as I am sure our post cards have indicated, a wonderful guide. David Heath-Nesbitt is one of the nicest, most intelligent, kindest, handsome men I've ever met! (And both my late husbands were not bad looking, so I can speak with some authority!) We have developed a real, well, for lack of a better word, affection for each other. What should I do about it? Help! I'm seventy-three, Vinnie, and too old to take on another husband. Aren't I? I know I cannot stay over here, and yet I enjoy his company so much I hate to leave him. He is not totally against coming to Virginia but I can see he is not happy thinking about it. Ah me, I feel almost like a teenager pouring out her problems of the heart! Wish you were here to talk with, but you're not. It has helped me to put this down on paper. I think I know where I'm heading now. Got to run; think I hear Ellie returning. She always bursts into the room with such exuberance I'm almost knocked off my feet!

Love, love in great haste ...

... Rose.

26

"Rose, have I thanked you more than a hundred times in the past hour for having the Currie save our rooms? I can't wait to sink my tired body into that bed." Ellie Johnson opened the door to their room and slumped into the nearest chair.

"Up, Ellie," commanded Rose. "You know what happens if you sit down. You'll never get up and put on your nightie. I'll even let you have the bathroom first."

"Go ahead, Rose," she moaned. "I'm so tired my teeth ache."

"Well, small wonder. You and Bob Lesley were talking a mile a minute all the way in from Oxford. What in the world did you two find so fascinating after nearly three weeks of traveling together?"

"His life, my life. Not so fascinating as interesting. Did you know that his parents had been missionaries? Bob was born in North China, in a mud hut. And his mother and Pearl Buck were friends and … do you really want to hear this Rose?"

"Frankly, Ellie, not at this hour. You sit; I'll finish in the loo and then it's yours." Rose had slipped out of her travel clothes and hustled into the bathroom.

When both women were settled in their beds Rose reached over to switch off the bedside lamp.

"Shall I leave a wake-up call for morning? Peter will have the Hummer here at nine sharp. What do you think?"

"We haven't failed to wake up at dawn yet, Rose. Why would tomorrow be any different? No, don't bother with a call."

"I agree. Ready for me to turn off the light?"

"Leave it on a bit longer, Rose. I feel like talking after that glorious soak and I don't like talking in the pitch black. I like to look at people when I'm speaking to them. I'm alone often enough in the dark at home. Home! Can you imagine *me* calling Wynfield Farms home? It sure is, though, and I sort of miss the place. How about you?"

"I confess I'm beginning to miss it too, Ellie. Well, to be honest, I have mixed emotions. I miss Annie, and I really miss old Max. Yet there is so much we haven't seen or done yet, and so much I want everyone to experience while we're here. But I know in my bones it is time to head home: we're ready. Have you heard that old saying that 'trouble comes in threes?' Our third spot of trouble was Charlie breaking his leg. Tells you something, doesn't it?"

"It tells me that you are human, Rose McNess, and as tired as I am. And it also tells me that you've done a superb job of shepherding us old fogies in and out and around England these past two and a half weeks. Think of the dreadful things that might have happened! For instance, Henrietta looking the wrong way crossing Brompton Road and being smacked by a double-decker bus, or Esther stumping a toe on one of those crumbling steps in any number of castles we've toured. Or Bob

Jenkins breaking a leg on a cobblestone in Canterbury. Now that would be what I call *trouble*."

"You're right there, Ellie. I would have picked Bob as candidate for some disaster. Thank heavens, so far he's healthy and mobile. And I must say I have to chuckle when I think of how Father Charlie broke his leg. Did you get the scenario on film?"

"Oh, Rose, didn't I tell you? Bob Lesley and I were watching from the footbridge so we had a bird's eye view, if you pardon the pun! Charlie started to sort of stretch and jump from his punt to the dock and a damned egret zoomed right in front of him. I guess that's what caused him to twist his leg as he landed. Poor Charlie! He sat there laughing at himself. Laughing until he realized he couldn't move his right leg. Did the doctors give you all the details? I heard you telling the others but I didn't get everything you said."

"It was a serious break, both bones of the lower leg. Two screws and plaster up to his thigh. Bi-something or other; at this hour my tired brain can't compute the medical terms. But his surgeon said Charlie was in wonderful condition and came through beautifully. Thanks to his vigorous exercising and walking at home I suppose. He'll be brought to Gatwick by ambulance on Friday and fly home with our group. I hated to leave him this afternoon but he looked fairly chipper. Had a nice room, pretty nurses coming and going, and David saw to it that he had plenty to read. Still, I'm nervous about his flying home so soon after surgery."

"Well, we do have a doctor with *us*, Rose, and I'm sure you've ordered wheelchairs at the other end, haven't you?"

"Oh, yes, rather, David was handling that. And in three days Charlie should be a lot more comfortable than he is tonight. I hate that he'll miss our day at the Globe tomorrow, and the theatre tomorrow night. *And* the farewell dinner on Thursday. But, as I said before, Charlie Caldwell rather than anyone else. I shudder to think if it had been Bob Jenkins."

ALMESBURY ABBEY

"Speaking of Bob, I think this trip has changed his life. Rather, his lifestyle. Have you noticed his color? He actually looks healthy for the first time. I bet when we return to Wynfield he'll be up with the sun. Probably want to walk with you and Max. No more 'the Prowler!' "

"Please don't speak of Max, Ellie. That really makes me long for home. To deliberately change the subject, my friend, did you enjoy your day at Blenheim and the Cotswolds?"

"It's a blur to me now, Rose. But yes, I did enjoy every minute. Wish I had known more about the Marlboroughs and the Churchills before I went to Blenheim but it was still dazzling. And the little Cotswold village where we stopped for lunch was out of a picture book. Just precious, with thatch-roofed toy houses and a stream burbling through the hedges and gardens."

"Which village was it, Ellie?"

"Gosh, you know I'm terrible on names, Rose. Something like bourbon and water. I am fairly good at word association!"

Rose giggled. "Good associating, Ellie. You must have been in Bourton-on-the-Water. Your description is perfect."

"That's it! Typical Cotswold. But my mind keeps returning to Wynfield Farms. It seems as if we've been gone a year. Don't you wonder what they are doing back there without us? No one to stir up trouble or rattle Miss Moss! Have you heard any news other than the one fax?"

"Not one peep. But I told my family not to write. You know how long it takes mail to get here if indeed it does get here. And I didn't expect Kate to send more than the one fax.

Ellie, the more I reflect on our trip the more remarkable it has been. Remember my telling you—right when you arrived at Wynfield—my own personal philosophy that life is one big tour? And that I was the tour *leader*? Well, that first day in London I had moments of panic. Here I was escorting ten virtual strangers in and out of one of the busiest cities in the world. Was I crazy?

BOURTON·ON·THE·WATER
COTSWOLD

GLASTONBURY ABBEY

NENE RIVER
FOTHERINGHAM

I had never really traveled with any of this group. But everyone is a treasured friend now. Looking back, this trip has changed everyone's life. For the better."

"Be careful how you phrase that, Rose. Father Charlie's life doesn't fit the category of 'better' at this stage."

"Maybe not now. But he always wanted to experience punting and he accomplished that. And his accident, though terrible, is not exactly life-threatening. As he recuperates at home he'll have time to do the reading he's always wanted to do. We've talked about Bob Jenkins and how healthy he seems. And look at Bob Lesley. Our good doctor has developed a real knack of meeting people. The British love him! Not that he was ever shy, but he's come out so much. And he's a delight. Confidence: that's what this excursion has given people, Ellie. A renewed sense of self-confidence. We seniors sometimes get so dependent on others: children, friends, caregivers. This trip has made us all free as birds."

"Shall I get the light, Rose?" asked Ellie, sleepily.

"Not yet, Ellie; now I want to talk. Take the Puffenbargers.

Harriet has always been in Henrietta's shadow. Now she's a star. Her adventure in the V&A has done wonders for her personality. And Henrietta is so proud of her!"

"How true," Ellie murmured.

"And would you have ever thought Frances Keynes-Livingston could be fun? I think she's enjoyed being a part of a group rather than leading one. And she keeps talking about the professor in Chelsea; I think she's got a crush on him!"

"Ummmm."

"Which brings me to Lib and Arthur. What do you make of them, Ellie? They seem perfectly content in each other's company, yet they don't cling to each other all the time. Just have to wonder what will happen when we do get back to Wynfield Farms."

"Don' know," came the drowsy response.

"And you've blossomed, Ellie. You've been so cheerful and such fun to be with every day. When I got nervous, your even disposition calmed me down."

"Psshaw, Rose. I was merely happy to be your roommate."

"Yes, Ellie, we've proved that we can still get around by ourselves, thank you very much. And get more out of a trip like this than when we were younger."

"I wouldn't have been interested in a trip like this when I was younger."

"And I—we—could not have afforded a trip like this! Raising children, thinking about college educations. Heavens! Flying to Europe was the same as flying to Mars as far as we were concerned."

"Uh-huh."

"One of the benefits of growing older, Ellie," continued Rose in spite of her roommate's drowsy responses, "is that as we change hopefully we're flexible enough to adjust to and enjoy the changes in the world around us. I predict that we'll return and find things pretty much the same in our own small house. All this newly-acquired self-confidence will help us settle back contentedly in our familiar corners. Except for that new 'public room' that Arthur has to name and decorate. We'll have to christen it. Think it will corrupt the morals of us OAPer's, Ellie?"

"Rose, since I cannot get you to stop talking, may I suggest a wee dram of brandy to help us both get to sleep? I have the dregs of a rather good bottle that has to go before we leave London."

"Ellie, I apologize. You got me all wound up! Yes, I'd love a drop. For medicinal purposes only, you understand. And I commend you, Ellie. You have not mentioned David tonight."

"I'm not going to, Rose. By this time I hope you know I'm a good listener. Of course I'm dying to know if he's asked you to marry him. Or if he *will* ask you. When and if you get ready to talk, I'll be here. Now, let this Old Age Pensioner hobble over to fetch the bottle of brandy and come to the aid and succor of her kindred spirit!"

~ ~ ~

GRITTLETON CHURCH
from
THE CHURCH HOUSE — EARLY MORNING

Canterbury Cathedral
from the Garden

THE CURRIE STREET HOTEL
Founded 1899

London

Dear Vinnie,

How I wish you were here! Sister is out
with Ellie Johnson and Rose so I am alone for
the afternoon and decided I would just sit
down and write to you. How are you feeling?
Has warm weather finally come to Wynfield?
Arthritis better? And did you get your eyes
checked? If the telephone rates were not so
expensive I would give you a call; I miss our
morning chats. But this rambling letter will just
have to suffice. We—that is, every one of us— has
said more than once that we miss you, and the
Major. You would add so much to our little
group.

I wish I could tell you <u>everything</u> that we
have done and seen but there would never be
enough time for that! Rose is doing a perfectly

wonderful job of leading us around. Of course she does have help! And the guide she hired is the nicest young man you've ever wanted to meet. I say 'young' advisedly; of course, everyone is younger than I am! But Mr. Heath-Nesbitt is around 70 I should imagine; younger than Rose, I can tell you that! But she seems quite smitten with him, and _he with her_! And this is not _just_ my opinion. I am seriously wondering if Rose will come home _alone_. Or, maybe not come home! Now please don't breathe this to a soul there at Wynfield. I am sure each of us on the tour thinks like I do, but we do not want to start rumors. But they are two fine people and I am happy they have found each other!

I told you I was going to ramble on a bit; here I am on page 2! Well, I won't go into detail about Sister's adventure at the Victoria and Albert Museum. Fortunately it turned out happily but she was lost in there for 6 or 8 hours! Can you imagine my worry? But she is none the worse for wear and chipper as a housecat now.

Rose gave us excellent advice on packing and I am glad I brought the sweaters and woolens that I did. Cool here but the days are clear and bright. The British tell us how lucky we are as it could be dreadful. The one thing I wish I had brought with me is my feather duster. You remember, the right wing of a goose that I keep in my apartment at home. I know you've seen it as you've commented on it. The British Museum could surely use a dozen of those wings; never have I seen such dust on many of those exhibition cases. I chatted with the guards about that and they agreed with me; said they were sorely understaffed in the cleaning department. Everyone we've met has been so pleasant. The English are well, civil. Perhaps a bit reserved at first, but once you've talked for a while, they "open" up. Do you know what I'm trying to say?

Well, dear, dear Vinnie, I have rambled on too long. I'll just fix myself a cuppa as they say and stretch out a bit and wait for the others to return. And I'll mail this on our way out to supper this evening. I believe Rose has made reservations for us at an old restaurant near Shepherd's Market. Rose does know more about London than anyone I've ever known!

Lots of love and affection <u>to you and your Major</u>,

Devotedly,

Henrietta.

27

Rose sat at the narrow writing desk. She paused, pen in hand, and pushed aside the curtains to look out of the window. The street outside the Currie was bustling with evening traffic, a noisy, dissonant yet lighthearted symphony. Street lights were twinkling on Brompton Road and through the garden she could see the lights of Harrods as they glowed into life in the fading dusk.

Was it three weeks ago I sat at this very window and looked out at an unfamiliar world? Why, it's my own neighborhood now. Where have the days gone? Have we really, as Henrietta insists, been to eight museums and six castles, including Windsor? And three street markets? And The Globe Theatre, that intriguing, enduring establishment. What a wonderful day yesterday turned out to be. What a wonderful day every day has been. Oh, glory, I hope Ellie and Esther use some caution in their last minute shopping spree. They know how jammed the underground gets after five.

Still, this was their decision and I refuse to worry about two grown women. Two senior women!

Rose returned to her notebook. She had kept meticulous notes throughout the three weeks and was updating them now. Dietary complaints, unsuccessful ventures, accidental discoveries, surprises. *I certainly count The Anchor as one of our crowning moments. Lunch where Samuel Johnson dined was a real high point for everybody. And didn't the crowd tuck into their steak and kidney pudding? How I loved seeing Bob Lesley forget his cholesterol completely. And Arthur! Talk about self-confidence! He was so proud to give us 'his' tour of the Globe. I believe they would have hired him if he'd agreed to stay in London. Amazing how much Shakespeare everyone remembered, probably from high school. Was it Frances who recited that long speech from King Lear? Yes, many surprises yesterday.*

"I better stop this daydreaming and concentrate on tonight and tomorrow," Rose said aloud. Seating arrangements had to be made not only for tonight's farewell dinner but also verified for the homeward flight. She consulted her small loose-leaf notebook: it was all there, alphabetically. Everett, Jenkins, Keynes-Livingston, Lesley, etc. Names, passport numbers, frequent flyer numbers, seats, number and descriptions of bags each person checked and/or carried.

That's the first thing I better ask about. How many extra cases are going home? I can't believe that after this last day of shopping everyone will return with just one bag. Menu preferences: one vegetarian, others, no specific choices. That's easy. There, that should do it. Just give me strength, dear Lord, to herd this group through Customs and onto that plane tomorrow morning. And no more broken legs, please.

Rose sat back in the lady's chair that doubled as a desk chair and thought of Charlie Caldwell. She had called him at the Oxford hospital this morning and he said cheerfully that "he felt like an Astronaut—'A.O.K.' " His only complaint was that he would miss all the spoiling he had been receiving, from the visits of kindly ladies from St. Giles Church to the over-abundant teas he had been consuming.

His last words to Rose had been reassuring. He was looking forward to rejoining the group at Gatwick. And yes, Bob Lesley had promised not only to pack his bag but would also check it through for him.

Rose told herself again that if one person had to have a calamity, Charlie Caldwell was the one. He is handling this with ease, as if broken bones were the norm and not the exception in one's life.

Charlie Caldwell's situation was in hand. *And as for tonight's dinner* ... The Currie Street Hotel had made their smaller Executive Dining Room available to Rose and her friends, and promised that an elegant dinner would be prepared for half-past seven. Rose had approved both menu and choice of wines and noted that the *maitre d'* had spared nothing for this special evening. Her first thought was that a simple supper would be sufficient to give everyone time to return to their rooms for final packing. How silly that was! In retrospect she acknowledged that Cyril had been absolutely correct in proposing this elegant bill of fare. The old gentleman favored Rose's Roamings as if they were the only guests in the hotel.

"With our pleasure, Mrs. McNess, we here at Currie Street wish to send you and your friends home with only the fondest memories of their stay in our country and especially in our hotel. It will be Chef's pleasure to prepare this farewell banquet. Not too heavy, to give the bad dreams, but not so light that our guests leave with a gnawing middle. They shall be pleased. And Zoe, in Housekeeping, insists on taking care of floral arrangements. That shall be our little gift to you, Mrs. McNess."

So no worries about dinner. I'll give David a few minutes for announcements, then I'll go over final details, and we should be back in our rooms by ten at the latest.

As Rose was finishing her notes and considering her dress for the gala evening Ellie burst into the room with her usual breezy gusto.

"Get me out of London, Rose, before I buy the city," she cried happily.

"Oh, no, Ellie, no more *stuff*!" said Rose, remembering Ellie's small, cramped apartment at Wynfield.

"Just kidding, ducks," teased Ellie, laughing. "I bought just one more Battersea box and then I did go overboard at that jeweler's in Camden Passage. I bought the watch fob I'd seen when we were there two weeks ago."

"You and Esther went all the way to Camden Passage? After Arthur's episode?"

"This underground is a snap, Rose, after you've ridden it once or twice. Did you know there are always little mice families playing on the tracks at Knightsbridge station? Anyway, Esther Jenkins is good company. A bit stuffy now and then but she does love to escape Bob's eye to shop!"

"And did she shop, or should I ask?"

"Did she! Esther bought herself a wig! She has been worrying about her hair as much as we have, Rose, only she didn't say anything about it until today. We treated ourselves to lunch at Marks & Sparks and she just, well, opened up. Confided *everything* to me. Said her hair had always been fine, but recently had started to disappear and what would I do? You know me, Rose, I'm an expert on wigs after my cancer left me as bald as Arthur Everett. I wasted no time in finding the best wig shop in London and off we went. Esther found one that is absolutely smashing. Well, smashing for *her*. So we celebrated by tooting off to Camden Passage. Now don't make a big deal out of this; it is so like her real hair that most people won't even notice. It is just fuller and more becoming. Promise you won't say much?"

"Solemn promise, Ellie. Did she make any other purchases after this great success of yours?"

"I'll say. But only the sensible-to-carry sort. Typical of Esther's good Pennsylvania stock. She found some lovely antique linen dinner napkins and two engravings she's going to save for Bob's eightieth. I've got those so he won't suspect. Everything packs flat, you see."

"I'm glad to hear that," sighed Rose. "That's one thing on my agenda tonight: how many extra bags we'll have going home with us. Poor Peter Bolt. Will the Yellow Canary be able to hold everything and everybody?"

"What time did you say dinner was tonight?"

"Half-past seven, Ellie, but Arthur and Lib have invited us for a drink in their room. And Arthur was very insistent that we be there at six-thirty."

"Jeepers! I forgot that. Sorry, I'll hurry."

"We both better hurry. Wouldn't do to be late for our own farewell party!"

~ ~ ~

Ellie and Rose dressed without speaking, sprayed on a final *poof!* of perfume and walked down the hall toward the lift.

"I'm sorry I cut it so close, Rose. I completely forgot Arthur's invitation."

"Just one of your 'senior moments,' Ellie," joked Rose, looking at her watch. "But we aren't late—it's six-thirty right now."

"I think only if the Puffenbargers had invited us for drinks would I be more surprised. Somehow Lib seems less social than the rest of us. Not that it matters. I like her. But you know what I mean. She's never had us in for drinks back in Wynfield so I certainly didn't expect it here. Maybe that dashing Arthur Everett has changed her."

"I'm sure of it!" giggled Rose. "Three weeks closeted with a Latin scholar would change anybody! Can you imagine their pillow talk?" They both giggled at the thought of this. "Perhaps this is their way of pouring oil on troubled waters, mollifying everyone's unspoken questions about three weeks of cohabitation. As if any one of us thought about it. I forgot as soon as I got over the shock of their telling me. Don't you agree, Ellie, that at our age nothing, absolutely nothing, is going to shock you? We've lived so long there is nothing predictable in religion, politics, economics and yes, morals. I just try to keep focused on my beliefs and let the meaningless wash over me."

"Sound thinking, Rose. And I agree. Remember my motto: 'Companionship beats coquetry.' I could care less if they had shared one room or two."

They laughed as they descended in the ancient lift that managed to stop with a hiccuping jolt on the third floor. Rose and Ellie found that they were the last arrivals and their fellow travelers greeted them with raised glasses and hearty greetings.

"Sorry everyone, my fault we're late," cried Ellie.

"It was my blameless roommate I *must* blame this time. But I see everyone else was punctual as usual. You really have been extraordinary these past weeks. Oh, David, I'm so glad you're here. I wasn't sure you'd get back until the dinner."

David Heath-Nesbitt looked particularly handsome this evening in his uniform of tweeds and college tie. But the suit was a new, or seldom worn one, and the shirt beneath the jacket was a pale blue that contrasted nicely with the stripes of the necktie. He was a man of languid, natural grace who obviously made his tailors more than content with their handwork: his clothes fit his lanky frame as easily as boats fit into slips. He caught Rose's words and came over to where she stood. Bowing slightly he looked into her eyes.

"My dear Rose, I would not have missed one second of this last evening with you and your delightful friends. And, I sincerely hope, now my friends as well. This is indeed, a night to remember."

Ellie and Frances Keynes-Livingston shot glances at one another and raised eyebrows in wonder. The remaining group milled around the two guides and tried to smile nonchalantly at the courtly scene played out before them.

Rose sensed the air of expectancy in the room. *If they think I'm going to make some announcement about David and myself they have another think coming!* Rose deliberately engaged David in a discussion of college colors and the 'Gaudy Night' formalities at Oxford. She managed to act oblivious of her friends' kind stares and unspoken words. Good natured, easy conversation soon resumed, along with the enjoyment of preprandial drinks.

"Which was your favorite: Cambridge or Oxford?"

"Do you favor the Bate's play or the one by Tom Stoppard?"

"Think we'd ever get the cook at Wynfield to fix cheese rarebit like we had at the Anchor?"

Rose was talking to David and half-listening to the conversational swirl when Arthur Everett rapped on his glass.

"Ahem," signaled Arthur in his quiet, commanding voice. "I wish to say, that is, Lib and I …" Here he faltered, as if looking for the precise nuance that his translations afforded him. "Ahem, that … Lib Meecham and I were married this past Monday in Oxford. *Mutandum manendum est.*"

The room was momentarily suspended in limbo. Ice cubes neither melted nor dropped. No bracelets clinked, no one coughed. It was as if everyone stopped breathing.

David Heath-Nesbitt finally broke the silence. It could not have lasted longer than thirty seconds but seemed more like an hour.

"Changing is remaining.... I beg your pardon, Arthur: you did *what?*"

"Lib and I were married this past Monday in Oxford. In the Town Hall. Presided over by both Father Charlie and the Town Magistrate. With Nigel as one of the witnesses. Jolly nice young man; promised to keep in touch after we get back to Virginia."

Now everyone talked at once, full of questions after the stunning announcement.

"Isn't anyone just plain happy for us?" asked Lib. Her sweet face held a look of bewilderment, as if she, too, could not believe what she had done.

Ellie, beaming, sidled up to Lib and whispered happily, "Of course we're thrilled for you, Lib. Tell me, did you plan this before you left Wynfield?"

Lib looked at Ellie and replied, with utmost composure, "Ellie, would you buy a pair of shoes before trying them on?"

"Oh, Lib, we're all so delighted for the both of you," enthused Rose. "It's just that ... we're totally shocked and surprised. How in the world did you pull this off? We were just in Oxford about a day and a half. When ... I simply can't take all of this in." Rose walked over to the low slipper chair and collapsed weakly onto it. Then she started to laugh, freely and happily.

"Lib, Arthur, I am so happy for you. Your marriage has made our tour a complete success!"

Everyone chimed in with felicitations. Glasses were refilled from the tiny corner bar and David Heath-Nesbitt gave a short and meaningful toast to the happy couple.

"*May the God who gives hope fill you with great joy. May you have perfect peace as you trust in Him.*"

"And that, my dear Lib and Arthur, comes from the fifteenth

chapter of Romans. One couldn't improve upon those words I daresay. Let me add how very happy I am for the two of you."

Frances Keynes-Livingston raised her patrician eyebrows and asked," Arthur, does this mean the end to our gin games back home? If so, I withhold my congratulations."

Arthur Everett beamed. "Indeed no, Frances. You know you're the best card player in Wynfield Farms. I did not marry Lib for her card sense. I shall still seek you out when I need a rousing gin game."

"Then let me add my congratulations to the many others," she smiled.

"Friends," called Rose, rising, and trying to be heard above the hubbub, "Cyril has promised us a veritable feast this evening and we dare not be late. Drink up and off we'll go. He's put us in the Executive Dining Room to the right of the Office. Let's continue our celebration down there."

The voluble group reluctantly ended their happy hour and slowly made their way to the stairs. *All of this exercise has made us OAPer's more limber*, Rose noted. *No one's complaining of bursitis or sprained knees. What a tour! And now this bombshell!*

Her thoughts were interrupted by David asking her solicitously, "Rose, may I have the honor of escorting you into dinner this evening?"

"You may, my good friend, with pleasure. This will *not* be your usual farewell dinner, I'm certain!"

~ ~ ~

28

It was nearly midnight and Kate Alexander, bundled in a terry-cloth robe with a towel wound around her clean, damp hair, had settled back on her couch to watch the late night television. She looked at her small apartment. A sea of boxes overwhelmed the tiny space.

No one can say that I'm not prepared to move, she thought. *Even though I have two more weeks here. Couldn't resist bringing these sturdy boxes home. Romero was heading to the dumpster with all of them. I hope I'm doing the right thing by going to Raleigh.* She worried the nail on her right thumb and finally gave up on the raggedy edge. *Of course I am! I've made my decision and that's that.* She was reaching for the TV remote when the jangle of the telephone startled her.

Who in the world could be calling at this hour? It's midnight. Mother wouldn't unless....

"Hello? Hello?" *Not another crank call, please.*

"Kate? Kate, it's Tom. Calling from San Francisco. Can you hear me? Do you want to hear me?"

"Tom Brewster! Now I can hear you, yes, now it's clear. Wh..what in the world are you doing? No, yes, tell me, because I am very tempted to hang up. You dropped off the face of the earth for three months. Go ahead, yes, I want to hear you."

Kate's towel tumbled to the floor spilling damp red hair around her flushed face. Her heart was beating crazily and she had trouble getting her thoughts together. Much less her words.

How can he do this to me? Tom Brewster is history! Waltzing back in my life at midnight. Who does he think I am? And why is my heart flip-flopping in my chest like a fish jumping out of a lake?

"Kate, I know I've been a real dog these past three months. But I couldn't call until I could offer you something. And now I can."

"Offer me something? What have you in mind?"

"Kate, will you marry me?"

Silence.

"Kate? Me, I'm offering you myself, in marriage. Say yes, oh, please say yes!"

"Tom, I'm … I'm speechless. You never wrote, you never called, you … and now … marriage?"

"Kate, you're all I thought of every day. But it wasn't fair to you to say anything until I got my life on course. I was hoping you'd feel the same way but obviously…."

"Oh, Tom, yes! Yes, I'll marry you! I've loved you since that first day in Wynfield Farms. But when…."

"Oh, darling, you've made my life complete. And I mean really complete. I'll sign up now for a married couples' apartment here at Stanford. I have a teaching fellowship for the next two years while I get my Master's and then if you're willing…."

"Willing to do what?"

"We'll return to Japan and I'll teach Creative Writing in my old school in Machida. How does that sound to you?"

"Oh, Tom, marriage sounds better. But when will you be home? Have I agreed to marry the vanishing Houdini? I have a bushel of questions to ask you."

"Kate, darling, I know you do. I'll be home in two weeks, and then I'll explain everything, I mean positively everything that I've been doing. Other than moping about you. Just trust me; I've been getting my life in order and deciding what to do with myself. Your 'yes' means I can get on with my plans. I mean, *our* plans. How does a June wedding sound?"

"Tom Brewster! It is practically May now! And I...." Suddenly Kate realized that her carefully selected job move to Raleigh meant nothing. She loved Tom and that fact erased all else in her life.

"Kate, do you mind keeping this a secret from Mom and Gan? I've got to study for a discussion group I'm leading and I don't have time to call them now. I'll try in the morning."

"Don't bother with your Grandmother, Tom. She's in England until this weekend. And I'd love to be the one to tell *her*. Don't wake up your parents at midnight. Sure, sport, if you've kept my love a secret for three months you can keep it quiet another night. You are serious, aren't you Tom? I won't wake up in the morning and find myself duped?"

"Darling Kate: I'm saner than I've been since coming to California. Why do you think I've waited so long? Why am I calling the most wonderful girl in the world at midnight to ask her to marry me? I have so much to tell you, so much to catch up on. But I really have to sign off now. Will you forgive me ... as well as marry me, my darling Kate?"

"Tom, do you remember the day you entered my life in the Reception Hall at Wynfield Farms? And you made me call your Gan and say she had a big package? Well, you are a big package of surprises, and I couldn't love you more. Despite the fact that you've made my life miserable these past three months. Yes, yes, yes I'll marry you, and in June. Just hurry back, please!"

Kate hung up the telephone and sat, dazed, for a long while. Then she did a barefooted dance all around the crowded rooms, kicking boxes as she cakewalked among them.

Who in Wynfield Farms could I tell? Would anyone be interested in romance? In marriage? Could they be? Oh, Rose McNess, how I'd love to talk to you right now. This may be the most unorthodox of proposals but it has made me the happiest woman in the world tonight. Good-bye Raleigh, hello California! I'm following my heart!

~ ~ ~

29

THE CURRIE STREET HOTEL
Founded 1899

Rose glanced around the small but elegant dining room. It
might well have been in one of the Georgian country estates
they had visited: silken wall coverings in muted shades of
celadon, tall windows, shuttered against the night with simple
swags of matching fabric highlighting their height, appropriate
corner pieces and serving buffets set against the walls. One long
table was placed parallel to the windows at the rear of the room
with a low, colorful centerpiece of anemones and freesia. Two
other round tables for four faced the long table. Tall, shining
candles gleamed; cutlery glistened on snowy damask.

"Oh, dear," Rose said half aloud, "I have forgotten place
cards."

"What is it, my dear?" asked David.

"Place cards. I forgot to make them."

"Heavens, Rose. That's the *only* thing you've forgotten. Let
everyone sit where they please. It all evens out. You and I must

sit here, of course. And Peter. He has been indispensable, don't you agree?"

"Oh, yes! But here's an extra place at the head table. Cyril must have miscounted. David, do you think you could say grace tonight? I've always counted on Charlie Caldwell at times like this. Poor Charlie...."

No sooner had the words flown out of Rose's mouth than she heard a whoop from the other travelers.

"Good evening, everyone!" came the shout from the doorway. There sat Charlie Caldwell, pale but dapper in blue blazer, gray flannels and plaster. Cyril, beaming beatifically, stood behind his wheelchair.

"Rose, you *know* I couldn't miss the farewell dinner! Particularly after the mischief I did in Oxford," he added sheepishly.

"If you mean the wedding you performed and blessed, yes, we've just heard about it!" replied Rose. "And we are thrilled! Almost as thrilled as your being here tonight! Did the doctors let you out or did you resort to bribing the nurses?"

"My surgeon, Dr. Powell, and the two others attending me, could find no fault in releasing me twelve hours earlier than scheduled. In fact, they suggested it. Said travel to London, getting settled, would be much easier on the old leg than rising up from the hospital bed and scooting straight away to Gatwick. So, here I am! And where is my happily married couple?"

"Ah, Charlie," spoke Arthur Everett with affection, "we are so glad you are back among us. What a day you had in Oxford, eh?"

"Didn't he though?" piped up Ellie. "I think I got your long stretch on film, Father. If it comes out, I'm sending it to Episcopalians Worldwide, if there is such an organization."

"All right, friends, since we do have Father Charlie back, let's put him to work. Charlie, you're here with us. Thanks to Cyril and his secrecy! On the end, so you won't be cramped. Would you mind giving us a short invocation tonight?"

"You know I'll be happy to, Rose. Let us bow our heads, please.

Dear Heavenly Father, who provides us with this bountiful food we are about to enjoy, and the lively friendship we shall enjoy, and have enjoyed, we offer our grateful thanks. And we thank you, Father, for this very large world and what this trip has been for each of us, in its diverse ways. For new sights seen, for unique experiences shared, for rare understanding of our heritage, for hearts that have blossomed and flowered into genuine love, we give our humblest thanks. We beseech of You to grant us safe passage as we return to our home and share our blessings in a most benevolent manner. Keep us from being boastful and prideful and above all, mindful of Thy love. All of this we ask in Thy name, O heavenly Father, Amen."

Each of the travelers echoed Father Charlie's "Amen."

"Thank you, Charlie," whispered Rose, leaning to her left and whispering in his ear. "That was just what we needed: a prayer for safe passage."

The evening was a resounding success. Cyril's menu and the Chef's talents left nothing to be desired. The *veal forestiere* was as succulent as promised. The sea bass soufflé caused gasps of delight when two young waiters paraded in with it and portioned it out to each of the guests. Course followed elegant course, accompanied by wine after wine. Just when the Wynfield Farms' crowd was groaning with satisfaction, Cherries Jubilee, flaming brightly, was paraded around the room. Accompanied by thick coffee and an offer of brandy on the side.

As everyone finished dessert and sat toying with coffee cups Rose stood and rapped her spoon against her water glass.

"Ladies, gentlemen, if this weren't so much fun I might be weeping at our farewell dinner. But Cyril has seen to it that we don't have time to be sad. I know you all want to join me in a

large round of applause for Cyril and his tireless staff!" The thir-
teen people in the room (save Father Charlie in his chair) rose
as one and gave the loyal Cyril a resounding vote of approbation.

"And a round, too, for Peter Bolt and David. I know we'll see
them tomorrow morning but we'll be in such a rush ... Peter,
David, what can I say? You each have made our trip so very special. We have a small token of great appreciation for each of you.
If my assistant will now come forward...."

Ellie Johnson walked to the head table bearing two large and
handsomely wrapped packages.

"Peter, this is for you, from each of us. And David, for you. It
is permissible to open them now; everyone is curious to see, I
know. And while they are unwrapping things, my friends, let me
tell you how wonderful you have been these three weeks.
Prompt, efficient, surprising: I'm out of adjectives. Please note
that not once have I called you 'folks,' as you might hear at
home. Nor have I nor anyone else in my hearing referred to you
as 'cute,' 'spry' or 'perky': three appalling adjectives! Even the
few worries you caused me fade into the sunset when I remember all the laughs we shared! Now, one more word as a tour
director, for I retire very shortly as such. Please have your bags
outside your door at seven sharp. Peter will be here to collect
them before breakfast. And yes, I've requested porridge again in
the morning. Cook assured me they'll have it. And kippers, for
you, Bob Lesley. Bags out at seven, breakfast, come down at 8:15
with keys in hand. And David and I'll take over from there. Any
questions?"

The group looked euphoric. Good food and good wine had
done its work.

"Wonderful. And so to bed. I'll see you all at breakfast. Thank
you, thank you, again."

"Say, Ms. McNess," yelped Peter Bolt. "I wantcha all to'noo,
you've been a grand buncha Yanks! And me hat is perfect.

Thankee!" Peter Bolt's face was ruddier than ever. He modeled the group's present, a soft leather driving cap from a smart shop in Burlington Arcade. His pride in owning such a cap was apparent.

"And I, too, my friends, wish to thank each of you. This has been a remarkable experience: one OAP leading a group of like comrades. And to you, Rose, what can I say? One of your sketches of my old college! When did you have time to do it? And get it framed? I'm simply ... overcome. Nothing has touched me so much. Thank you dear friends. I shall see you in the morning and ride with you to Gatwick. Sleep well tonight and know that Peter and I both are touched by your generosity. Cheerio, all!"

One by one the group slowly unfolded stiff knees and left for their rooms. Ellie and Frances Keynes-Livingston walked out together, chatting quietly with Father Charlie. Bob Lesley helped push his roommate down the hall toward the lift. The love birds had been the first to depart, and the Puffenbargers and the Jenkins were not far behind.

A conspiracy, Rose noted, *to leave me alone with David.*

"David, you've given so much these past three weeks. If I don't have another chance in the morning, I want you to hear it from me now: thank you from the bottom of my heart."

"Rose, what can I say? Except to perhaps quote Arthur: *Mutandum manendum est.* I won't open old chapters, but my offer still stands. I am more convinced than ever. Have you thought about my offer?"

"Oh, David, more than you know. And I'll give you my answer in the morning. Good night, my dear friend and colleague." With that Rose stood on the tips of her toes and gave David Heath-Nesbitt a warm and genuine kiss on his cheek.

~ ~ ~

30

"It surely does feel good to be situated at last," grumbled Ellie, settling into her seat on the aisle. "I thought we'd never get off the ground. Where did all those last-minute people come from, Rose?"

"I have no idea. Some ill-disciplined tour group that didn't listen to their guide and tried to cram on with umpteen carry-ons. I'm glad they made them go back and check each of them, even if it does mean a late departure. Not one of our group was guilty of that!"

"Can you believe this adventure is nearly over? Why, it will be almost May when we get home. Spring will be in full bloom." Ellie smiled at the thought, eyes sparkling.

"What a pleasant thought: two Springs in two months."

"And in the Spring," mused Ellie, "a young man's fancy and all that stuff. Come on, Rose, we're in the air. Tell your old roommate about you and David. Just the facts, ma'am."

Lowering her voice and turning to face her friend, Rose said evenly, "There is nothing to tell, Ellie, really. We met, we had a marvelous three weeks together—in your presence I might add—and we said good-bye. *Also* in your presence. End of story."

~ ~ ~

Rose managed to keep her face a mask of normalcy as she spoke to Ellie. But in Gatwick it had been a different story. Rose felt a sharp *pang* whenever her eyes met David's.

David Heath-Nesbitt was at her side driving from the Currie Street Hotel to the airport and assisting everyone off the 'yellow canary' for the last time. He worked with Rose to smooth the wrinkles out of the departing procedures. When Peter Bolt had pushed Father Charlie's chair as far as he was allowed to do so in the Boarding area he returned and once again shook Rose's hand warmly and boomed: "Yer the tops, Ms. McNess. Be sure'n come back soon!" Then, to David, "I'll move the 'canary,' Guv, over to the usual. Be waitin' for ye there."

"That's what we liked about Peter. No going on and on about nonsensical matters. And now, it's time for our good-byes, David. And it is good-bye. I did think about your offer of marriage, dear David. You know my philosophy; how many times have we talked about it? Life is like a tour bus, or a cruise ship as Ellie prefers to think of it. But it's also a fanciful, fantastical adventure, where romance sometimes happens for the lucky ones. You and I were lucky. But in our case, we're both changing buses, transferring to different routes at this junction. Our time together has been special David, but now my bus is moving on again. With me. My answer has to be no...."

He interrupted her with a finger to her lips. "No going on about nonsensical matters, Rose McNess. I knew what your answer would be. I think I knew the moment I asked you to marry me. I *need* you, but that is selfish of me. I'm one more man and there are ten other people who need you even more than I. And no telling how many more back in…."

"Wynfield Farms."

"Yes. I can tell how you light up their lives, my dear. You have that rare spark of stardom, a vitality that changes everyone. Oh, I envy them, Rose McNess. Envy them and I am jealous of them. But this interlude we've shared is a jewel that I shall unwrap and polish when I get that case of…. What *did* you call it, Rose?"

"The gloomies. We old folks are prey to the gloomies now and then."

"Yes, the gloomies. Well, I shall remember and treasure our hours together whenever I suspect the gloomies are coming upon me. You've denied me marriage; surely you won't deny me a farewell kiss?"

They embraced and kissed warmly. Both wiped a bit of moisture from their eyes as Rose turned to hurry toward the plane. She could not speak and her smile was wobbly as she turned and waved.

~ ~ ~

"Think you'll ever see him again, Rose?" persisted Ellie.

"Probably. No, make that *possibly*. My hairbrushes do wear out rather frequently. And I'd certainly recommend David as a guide."

"You mean you'd share him? That divine man? Oh Rose, really!" Ellie rolled her eyes in mock horror.

"Ellie, you are the absolute limit. I am going to look down upon Ireland and then I am going to rest my eyes. Suddenly I am exhausted. Father Charlie, are you all right up there?" Rose leaned forward and spoke to Charlie Caldwell who fortunately had the entire seat in front of them. David had pulled a few strings with the Captain to manage this feat.

ST. KEVIN'S "KITCHEN" AND ST. KEVIN'S TOWER
(CHURCH)
GLENDALOUGH, IRELAND

Joyce Tower (a Martello Tower)
Sandy Cove —
Ireland — overlooking
Dublin Bay on the
Irish Sea

"Snug as a bug, Rose. Couldn't be better. Don't plan to move until I have to. I'm going to sleep most of the way, but don't want to close my eyes until after they serve lunch. Or supper. Why, it's early afternoon and I'm making plans for supper. It will take me another three weeks to undo my British habits."

"I think we'll all sleep after the meal. And I promise I'll put a muzzle on Ellie so she won't talk to you. Despite your accident, Charlie, would you consider the trip a success?"

"First class, Rose. Best yet! Perfect hotel, superb guide and driver, great companions, unexpected delights along the way. My broken leg was hardly a blip on the screen. Except for the three days 'in hospital,' as they say over here, I didn't miss a trick."

"As I said when this happened, if anyone could survive such a disaster with poise it was you, Charlie. Thank the good Lord Bob Jenkins came through in one piece."

"He's not back in Wynfield Farms yet, Rose," piped up Bob Lesley who had been listening to the conversation.

They laughed and then relaxed, enjoying the final lap of Rose's Roamings.

~ ~ ~

It was twilight when the eleven weary travelers arrived at the front door of Wynfield Farms. The April air was soft and sweet. The tall poplars, almost in full leaf, were blowing to and fro as if they were greeting the returning residents with giddy bows of welcome.

Rose had ridden up front with Romero and was the first out of the Wynfield van.

"Here we are! Rose's Roamings have made it safely home. And does it look good! Here, Henrietta, let me give you a hand. Wait a second, Harriet, I'll help you, too. Those knees are going to stiffen up tonight, I guarantee it."

The exhausted group straggled out of the van, bleary-eyed and punchy.

"Always good to go but great to get home," sang Bob Lesley enthusiastically. "Hold on there, Charlie. Romero and I have a plan to get you inside. Just a moment."

Romero had begun to untie the pile of suitcases from the van's rack and the group was more interested in his success, or lack of it, than moving forward into the Reception Hall.

"Welcome to Wynfield Farms! Welcome to Wynfield Farms!" Miss Elvina Moss, dressed in classic navy pinstripes, stood in the doorway with arms outstretched.

"Now I know I'm back," whispered Ellie. "Would you look at that: Mother Hen clucking to her wandering chicks."

"It's her way of trying, Ellie," replied Rose. "Let's give the old girl a warm greeting. She may have even missed us." As cheerfully as she could, Rose cried, "Thank you, Miss Moss. We're happy to be here." *I cannot bring myself to say that I'm happy to see her. But I do feel a deep sadness after what I've learned.*

"Mrs. McNess! Mrs. Johnson! Dr. Lesley! Father Caldwell … what in the world?"

Kate had now come out to stand by Miss Moss.

How good to see Kate, thought Rose. *She looks prettier than ever! And she's the only one who can tell us what has been going on in this place!*

"Kate!" chorused many of the voices. "So good to see you!"

Romero had radioed for Ernest and the two of them lifted Father Charlie bodily up the steps and into the Reception Hall where he gratefully sank onto one of the Chippendale benches by the door. The tour group was now chattering happily and identifying bags to be brought up to their apartments. Other residents had come down to join in the commotion. Everyone had a kiss for Kate and the Puffenbargers engaged Miss Moss in a lively conversation about a few of the extraordinary sights they had seen. It was altogether so quietly confusing for ten or fifteen minutes that no one even noticed the attractive Afro-American woman with closely cropped hair sitting at the Reception Desk.

Miss Moss found her opening and seized upon it. "Ladies, gentlemen, those of you returning. If I may, please ..." She strained to capture the attention of the entire group that refused to stop gabbing at full steam.

"While you are gathered together, this must suffice as a meeting. I would like to introduce my successor, Mrs. Paula Gallentine. Rhymes with Valentine. Would you please stand, Mrs. Gallentine?"

Mrs. Gallentine stood, all six feet of her. She smiled, and her chocolate-brown face was beguiling. Then she bowed shyly. Turning to Miss Moss and speaking in a voice husky and warm said, "I think what this group needs is a good night's sleep. I look forward to meeting each of you tomorrow."

The returning travelers were rooted to the Oriental rug. After three weeks absence, ten hours flying, minds and bodies topsy-turvy with trans-Atlantic time tables, this was a change in the old homestead. Romero had not hinted at it in the drive from the airport. Miss Moss's announcement was an unexpected thunderbolt.

"Well," yelped Ellie, never one to be silent for long, "what do you know?"

"I am dumb struck," whispered Rose. "Mrs. Whozit is right: what we need is a good night's sleep. Talk about changes...."

"And the public room, Miss Moss," asked Arthur Everett, "how is that progressing?"

"Oh, very well, Mr. Everett, very well. As far as I can see, you understand."

"I should like to announce at this moment," he continued, "that I am prepared to name this room."

"Well done, Arthur," cried Bob Lesley. "And his is the voice of authority, Miss Moss. While we were in England we named old Arthur the Chairman of the Pub Study Commission. Let's hear it, Arthur, what's it to be?"

"The Rose and the Grape," intoned the Chairman. "Thus we honor our eponymous, heroic tour leader *and* a bit of the bubbly. Objections may be entertained but not at this hour."

"Oh, Mrs. McNess," called Kate, "what a lovely thing for him to do! And I want to add further to that if I may."

"Kate, for goodness sakes, speak up! What else could you possibly add? For my part, I'm speechless!"

"Mrs. McNess and everyone, this is hard for me. But I promise not to cry. And my tale does have a happy ending if I should break down in the middle." Kate looked at the weary faces focusing on her every word. "You may remember I'm to receive my degree in two weeks. And I went ahead and made plans, even before Miss Moss told me of her relocation, to accept a position in Raleigh, closer to my home town. But since then, I've resigned that because ... because I'm going to get married!"

"Tom?" cried Rose.

"Tom Brewster!" returned Kate gleefully.

The entire room whooped with joy and Kate was embraced by all. Rose was not the only person who had tears streaming down her face. Lib whispered to Arthur, "Do you think we started a trend in Oxford, dear?"

"Kate, Kate, I'm thrilled," Rose managed to speak when she finally got her chance to hug the girl. "You'll truly be one of the family now! Didn't I tell you that my grandson was not only handsome but smart, too? Arthur, what is that Latin phrase you were spouting at the Currie? Can you remember it now?"

"Certainly, my dear. Only in this case I think I should perhaps alter the grammar to fit the occasion. *Mutare constans est manere*: To change is to remain the same. We don't change; things around us do."

"Change: that is what the world is all about. Thank you, Arthur. This tour continues to roll on, my friends," said Rose. "Miss Moss and Kate may be getting off at this stop but we'll go on! Mrs. Gallentine, hop aboard the bus. Life's challenges and adventures wait around the next corner!"

~ ~ ~

PHOTO BY W.A. DICKINSON

BARBARA M. DICKINSON

About the Author

Barbara Dickinson's first novel, the critically acclaimed *A Rebellious House*, reflects both her love for the State of Virginia and comprehension of the complexities of aging. In this, her sequel, she encourages her characters to explore the large world outside their "small house."

Barbara graduated from Wellesley College and received her Master of Arts in Liberal Studies from Hollins University.

A frequent contributor to the Book Page of THE ROANOKE TIMES, Barbara has also written and illustrated a children's book and a cook book.

When not traveling, Barbara Dickinson lives in Roanoke with her husband, Billy, and her Scottish terrier, Maxine.

~ ~ ~

To order additional books, please use coupon below.

Mail or fax to:

Brunswick Publishing Corporation

1386 LAWRENCEVILLE PLANK ROAD
LAWRENCEVILLE, VIRGINIA 23868
Tel: 804-848-3865 • Fax: 804-848-0607
www.brunswickbooks.com

Order Form

❏ *Small House, Large World* by Barbara M. Dickinson
$19.95 ea., paperback .... $ _____

❏ *A Rebellious House* by Barbara M. Dickinson
$24.95 ea., hardcover .... $ _____
$19.95 ea., paperback .... $ _____

Total, books .... $ _____
VA residents add 4.5% sales tax .... $ _____
Shipping – $5.00 first copy .... $ _____
    $.50 ea additional copy .... $ _____

Total .... $ _____

❏ Check enclosed.

❏ Charge to my credit card:
    ❏ VISA   ❏ MasterCard   ❏ American Express

Card #_____ Exp. Date _____

Signature: _____

Name _____

Address _____

City_____ State_____ Zip _____

Phone # _____